Blue Lady's MISSION under FIRE

I0584424

A STORY OF LOVE, LIFE & SURVIVAL

The Angelica Mason Series, Book 3

STEPHANY TULLIS

USA TODAY Bestselling Author

" With nowhere to run and nowhere to hide, what can she do to survive?

Blue Lady's MISSION under FIRE (The Angelica Mason Series, Book 3)

Published in the United States by Diamond TK Publishing

Text Copyright @ 2019 Stephany Tullis

All rights reserved

PUBLISHER'S NOTE
This book is a work of fiction. Names, characters, places and incidents are products of the author's imagination or are used fictitiously.

Cover Design by Michelle Fairbanks, Fresh Designs
Adobe Stock images
2nd Edition

INTRODUCTION

It's all about the search for love and life purpose...

Blue Lady's MISSION under FIRE is Book 3 in *The Angelica Mason Series* (There are four books in this series). Book 5, Blue Lady's SEARCH for LOVE will be available in the Spring of 2023). The books revolve around a common theme—the search for love and life purpose.

Which is more important or are they interrelated?

She's already sacrificed her career… must she now sacrifice her life?

The MISSION changed. Her COVER is blown.

In Blue Lady's MISSION under FIRE, Angelica Mason, (aka, The BLUE LADY), along with her faithful sidekick Jonathan C. Jarewski (JaRew), face new challenges and stare down old demons.

When Angelica is fired by her ex-boss, the Mayor of her hometown, Smoothville, Georgia, she eagerly accepts her mentor's offer to serve as his project manager on a controversial federally funded demonstration project.

Angelica confronts her first challenge on Day 1 when she arrives in Washington, D. C. and learns that the feds cut the funding for her position. She is now one of six hand-picked street organizers who will be working undercover in Upstate New York. When smooth talking private investigator Dez Cooke makes himself quite at home in the first project team meeting and knows more about the planned project than she does, Angelica discovers she is face to face with challenge number two.

By the end of the first official briefing session, Angelica learns that a new murder case is added to the growing list of homicides in upstate New York. And this time, two teenagers are killed. Instead of celebrating the 4th of July, another community vigil is held to celebrate the dead. Challenge three.

Community leaders call another meeting. But no one has any answers. Challenge four.

And Angelica quickly learns that this is only the beginning.

It starts with a round of tequila shots and a hip swiveling line dance. Did Angelica hear the shots before she felt the shove? Was it an accident? Or was she the target?

In the third book in *USA Today* bestselling author Stephany Tullis' Angelica Mason Series, Angelica Mason and Jonathan Jarewski find themselves in a MISSION under FIRE.

The Angelica Mason Series:

BLUE LADY (The Prequel and short story)

Blue Lady's SWEET DREAMS, Book 2

Blue Lady's MISSION under FIRE, Book 3

Blue Lady's DÉJÀ VU on the Seas, Book 4

Blue Lady's SEARCH for LOVE, Book 5 (Available Spring, 2023)

DEDICATION

I dedicate this book to victims of gun violence and their families, and those community workers, advocates, and, others who struggle to find solutions to one of the biggest and most tragic issues facing African American communities.

Dear Friend,

Thank you so much for reading Blue Lady's MISSION under FIRE. This book has special meaning for me for several reasons. I'm from upstate New York and while the events in this book are totally fictional, the circumstances described are unfortunately more common than I prefer to think about. And although I wrote and published this book in 2019, inner city violence continues to flourish. I refuse to accept that it is the 'norm'.

Stay tuned for information of my upcoming partnership with local community organizations to sponsor my, 'Give Peace a Chance' initiative (A BLUE LADY project).

I love for you to share your thoughts. You can email me at: stephanytwrites@gmail.com or look for me on Facebook.

Happy Reading,

Stephany T.

ALTER EGO

"An alter ego means an alternative self–
which is believed to be distinct from a person's
normal or true personality."

VIOLENCE

"Behavior involving physical force intended to
hurt, damage,
or kill someone or something."

CONTENTS

CHAPTER ONE

"By the way, who the heck is this Dez Cooke?"

"GOOD MORNING. You must be Angelica."

"Good morning." I respond automatically to the unexpected visitor as the door closes behind him. Since he knows my name, I conclude he isn't in the wrong room. He parks a black Nike backpack in the corner chair. I feel overdressed in my quite casual, but neatly pressed khaki slacks and white blouse.

"And you are?" Despite *his* comfort level, I figure I'd better confirm he's in the right place. After all, tons of meetings take place in the Washington, D.C. Embassy Suites hotel and even though he knows my name, I'm a little nervous. His gray Nike Tech sweat suit, matching Michael Jordan cap and Air Jordan's, are not what you see in a typical *business casual* meeting.

"Hey! You can call me Dez." The owner of the raspy voice smiles, opens a bottle of water, and grabs a chocolate donut, making himself comfortable. Nothing like finding a total stranger in the meeting room where you expect to have a one-on-one pre-meeting briefing with your boss.

"Nice to meet you."

I follow Cooke's lead, opting for hot coffee, refusing to be tempted by the scrumptious looking assortment of breakfast items on the side table in the small suite. A comfortable loveseat, two cushioned side chairs, and a circular work table will more than meet our needs. A second table unit holds a forty-eight-inch-screen TV and a computer accompanied by a top-of-the-line laser printer. Three desk chairs complete our project office. I claim a seat at the desk, setting my laptop bag on one of the curved swivel chairs.

I love DC but never thought I'd return to work here. Nor did I think I'd ever be a part of another Beckham Johnson project. After all, I had jumped ship responding to the call of home and my high school sweetheart several years ago. Beckham and I had stayed in touch, though, and he remained supportive of me and my career. I'm truly thankful for his spur-of-the-moment offer for me to run his new project team on a recently awarded federal demonstration project. Beckham was more than a mentor. He was a good friend. And friends are hard to find these days. I'm lucky enough to have three really good ones. Beckham, my colleague Jonathan Jarewski—who had agreed to join me on this new assignment, and Nicole Honeywell, aka Nik, my BFF. If I had not known it before, I do now. They rallied to my support during my father's recent illness. I don't think I would have made it without them. So today, life is indeed good despite the unexpected start. I'm sure Beckham will fill me in on Cooke.

As I add cream to my coffee, the door opens and Beckham greets us, "Good morning. I see you two have met. Great. I'm glad you've had some time to get to know each other. Sorry I'm late."

Well, that answers that. *Someone* seems to have known that this pre-meeting included three people—not two as I'd expected. Now I'm even more confused. I don't know how Beckham and I can discuss project strategy with this Dez character here. I skim the meeting agenda I'd downloaded from my laptop last night as Beckham helps himself to coffee. I circle item #2. 'Project Strategy' with my red pen.

"So, have you guys had a chance to compare notes? Let's move to the table."

Compare notes about what? Though surprised, I bite my tongue and hold my question.

Tattoo-wearing Dez doesn't appear to be surprised at all. It's obvious that *he's* aware of the plan. That explains how he knew my name.

"Let's catch up."

My mentor sips from his coffee as though he has all the time in the world. That cinches it. Something's up. I stifle my escalating temper and desperately search for the objectivity and logic of what seems to be a big change of plans. After all, Beckham had pleaded with me to take this job. To lead this special federally funded project. Granted his offer came when I needed it most. A few months ago, I found myself jobless after requesting an extension to my family medical leave of absence from my Smoothville, Georgia City Manager position. Luke Evans, the Mayor and my boss insisted I return due to work requirements of my job. I refused citing that my father had not yet been officially released from his doctor. Luke responded to my plea by recruiting my ex, Shawn Mallory, to replace me.

Any doubts I had fizzled when he added, "You can trust me..."

The two chat as they move to the table. The weather. Cooke's flight. It sounds like he's from New York. Out of the corner of my eye, I see Beckham place three red folders on the table and pull out a third chair that I assume is for me. I don't move from the desk, checking my email for messages. I haven't heard from Jarewski yet. No email. But no news is good news. We have another hour or so before the official team meeting starts.

Jonathan C. Jarewski, aka JaRew, and I joined forces ten years ago. He stepped to the plate and helped me salvage Luke Evans' then crumbling mayoral reelection campaign. Luke appointed me as his city operations manager after he held onto his seat by the skin of his teeth. Jarewski and I worked so well together on the campaign that I made him part of my contract proposal to Luke and haven't regretted it yet. That's not to say that we see eye to eye on everything— far from it. I had to seriously twist his arm to get him to join me on this project.

"Did you see that play?" I frown as I tune in and quickly out of the early morning replay of the ninth inning of last night's showdown between the NY Mets and my home team, the Atlanta Braves, and close my laptop.

"Did you catch the game, Ange?"

"No, afraid not." *I was too busy preparing for this meeting,* I think, but don't bother to say.

Beckham doesn't acknowledge my response and continues his conversation with Dez, who seems to be his newfound buddy. "How's Linc, Dez?"

From what I can gather from the free-flowing exchange, Beckham called Lincoln Keyes, a retired NYS police officer, a well-respected lieutenant, and filled him in on the envisioned project, told him he was recruiting, and needed some experienced community-based types to round out his "technical team"—later translated to mean "community-based street team."

Keyes filled him in on his nephew, Desmond Cooke's background. He'd aced the trooper exam and was ready for training. At the last minute, the state police captain, Keyes's good friend, called to apologize. "There's nothing I can do, Linc." For some reason, the original check of Cooke's background was as clean as freshly fallen snow until the investigative team came across what was supposed to be a sealed conviction due to Dez Cooke's then youthful-offender status. The captain tried to pull a few strings, but some rules aren't meant to be bent.

Too much of a fighter to give up, Cooke carved a new career for himself doing what he had been trained to do. As a freelance private investigator, he had no shortage of clients and had been working independent cases across the country. Without giving Beckham any specifics, Linc urged Beckham to meet his nephew and find out for himself. Beckham flew to LA for a face-to-face meeting.

Cooke indicated that he should be able to close out a current high-profile case and be in DC the following week. They wrapped up their deal over the last week.

From the sound of it, Beckham hadn't had time to touch base with me. He'd spent all his effort working with his Department of Justice contact and his proposal writing staff to rework the project. Cannellini, the contact, confidentially shared with him that the amended proposal had been flagged by the powers that be as one to watch. He also confided, "You're good and know your stuff, but none of us know how you pulled this one together. And so quickly. Truthfully, I don't want to know." *I do,* I thought. And made a mental note to ask the question no one else seemed to want to ask.

He assured Beckham that the amended proposal was under lock and key. Now that statement got my attention and I decided to officially join the existing two-person exchange. Cooke asked, "So no one can believe you'd take something like this on? Impressive, BJ."

"Thanks, Dez, but I owe a lot to you and your uncle." I continue to be a nonparticipating but active listener.

"I hope you feel the same once we get started. We have to hit the ground running, you know?" His sudden quiet, somber-like demeanor spoke volumes.

Who the heck is this Dez Cooke?

For the first time since the meeting began, I became the center of attention. I realize the charms on my bracelets have been rattling against the edge of the desk as I wrote.

"You're not taking minutes of this meeting, are you, Angelica?"

"I'm not your secretary, Cooke!"

Beckham gives me a look I've never seen before but doesn't speak a word.

"I apologize. That's not what I meant."

I'm shocked by his apology but don't buy into Cooke's humble pie façade. He might fool Beckham, but not me. Something's going on, but I can't detect what—at least, not yet.

"What *did* you mean, Mr. Cooke?"

He surprises me again and responds with a lazy smile. "I meant that everything we do on this project has to be confidential. We need to talk about it as little as possible, even among ourselves. Once we go live, we won't know who's listening, whom to trust, and most importantly, who's watching whom."

Beckham interjects, "Before Cannellini ended his call, he told me that everyone on the federal review team and up the chain of command believes we're crazy to try this. Before I could ask him what he meant, the phone was dead. When I received the final sign off and contract, I noticed that all staffers from top to bottom were sworn to secrecy."

Cooke nods at Beckham's revelations as though he isn't surprised.

"We should probably do the same, BJ."

Beckham looks from Cooke to me. "What do you think, Ange?"

"I don't know what to think." *I don't have an opinion.* I feel like I'm shooting fiery darts in a pitch-black game room.

Cooke answers for both of us. "We need to have the entire team sign sworn confidentiality statements. If word of the project gets out on the street, we need to make sure it's not coming from anyone on the team."

I didn't bother to comment further. I feel like a cruise ship tender tossed by stronger-than-expected ocean waves.

Beckham rises, slowly walks to the door, and rattles the doorknob. After confirming that it's locked, he returns to the table, lowers his voice, and briefs me.

Cooke is working a *New York Times* crossword puzzle.

Beckham's muted, well-modulated public speaking voice interrupts my traitorous thoughts — but warns that something is indeed up. I've witnessed his practiced double entendre deliveries too many times not to recognize this one when it's directed at me. What is he not telling me?

"So, I apologize for the short notice, Ange. But I pulled this together at the very last minute." Cooke cracks his knuckles, picks up his pencil, and continues to work the puzzle. I can't help but notice he's almost finished.

Beckham continues, seemingly oblivious to the table games, but I know him too well. I'm sure he's enjoying every minute of the Cooke-Mason pregame.

"It looks like we have a tentative sign-off on the amended proposal, but we don't know the funding allocation. I do know we have an abbreviated timeline to get the street team on the ground. Dez and I think our proposed team of seven—that includes you and your colleague Jarewski—can handle this. When do you expect him, by the way? Is his plane on time?"

"He'll be here by eleven. Isn't that when we plan to start?" I figure I should clarify a few things since I have no idea where this is all going. The fact that I don't have any details on the amended project or the newly organized street team is no mistake. Beckham doesn't make mistakes.

"That's the plan. So, here's what I want to cover before the rest of the team arrives."

That settles that. He's already recruited the team. Cooke and I skim Beckham's short list of pre-meeting agenda items. My clinking bracelets and Desmond's knuckle-cracking shatter the silence.

"Did you guys see the headlines?"

Do I look like a guy? I stare ahead of me. Beckham shakes his head. "Which?"

"*The New York Times*. The governor has increased the funding allocation for New York's Gun Violence Elimination Program."

"You think we might be able to get a supplemental grant? Wow. Matching state funds might give us a bump on the federal budget, too. Perfect."

"Maybe. Don't know much about grants. Just thought I'd mention it." They both look at me.

"I can check it out." This is going to be interesting. I make a mental note to check with JL — Jocelyn Lopez, deputy mayor of Smoothville, a colleague of mine. She's from the Bronx and has friends on the New York City Council. As an afterthought, I text her. "Call me later. Ciao."

"Hey, Ange. This might be a good time for you to meet Linc."

"Linc?"

"Yes, Dez's uncle. Remember? As a retired NYS police officer, he still has a lot of contacts on the force. He might have some info on state grants. If he doesn't, I bet he'll know who will."

"Hey, Lady." I'm distracted when I notice for the first time that Cooke's ruined his pearly white smile with some kind of gold filling on his bottom teeth. He slides a business card across the table. "My uncle's number— cell and business. I'm sure he'll be happy to hear from you. He's good people, right, BJ?"

THE STREET TEAM is present and accounted for per Beckham. Desmond Cooke is to his left. I'm at his right. He's introduced us both to the others who sit with their donut and or bagel on a small paper plate alongside a folded napkin. Coffee seems to be the drink of choice.

Beckham doesn't explain what happened to the original project team. The one I'm supposed to be heading—or so I thought. Or, what its relationship is to the newly created street team. The perfunctory pre-meeting that I'd just sat through had not prepared me for this turn of events. Me on a street team? I don't know anything about street teams. And even less about what I'm supposed to do. I have a few words for Mr. Beckham Johnson after this meeting. Or should I say for 'BJ?'

Jarewski, directly across from me, pokes my foot under the table. I ignore his poke and his smirk. He knows I'm hot.

To JaRew's left, we have Jude Hinkley, a few years older than me. He's prematurely gray with sandy-blond hair and asks us to call him JB. *Just great. How are we to manage a team with a BJ and a JB?* He has green eyes, and unlike the rest of us, he's wearing a suit. Charcoal gray. It looks like he's going to church. Or, as I take another look, a courtroom might be his preferred place of business. He's nibbling on fruit snacks. He brought his own.

Marcus Pope arrived thirty minutes late and has not yet removed his dark Ray-Bans. The tiny diamond earring in his left ear is out of sync with his blue-and white tailored shirt and dark tie.

"Looks like everybody's here." *Oh, no, the heck we aren't!*

"Excuse me, but pray tell, can someone tell me why I'm the only female in the room?" I look at Beckham but make it clear that my question is open to the full cast of characters.

CHAPTER TWO

"Are you sure you want to do this?"

JAREW SNAPS ANOTHER SELFIE. Somewhat of a challenge since the towering, nineteen-foot Abraham Lincoln sits majestically behind us as though wisely watching our every move. I wonder what Honest Abe would think about Beckham's—newly christened BJ—behind-the scenes maneuvers. Funny thing is, I don't blame him for doing what he had to do to get the funding. Dang, I would have done the same thing.

Get that deal.

Work that deal.

But once I'd cut the deal, I would have been on my cell updating my project director—not replacing her with some PI with a major in street life.

JaRew knew about the deal changer before he made it to the hotel. I'd discreetly texted him during one of several premeeting exchanges between our illustrious leader and Dez Cooke. The hotel shuttle was late picking him up from the airport. He walked into the meeting room, dropped his black leather duffel on the floor and took the seat opposite me. When my male colleagues ignored my challenge about the all-male street team, I decided to do the same. Until I diversified our team. JL was a prime candidate, and I was counting on her to help me fill one vacancy. Also, I had no doubt that she could find me at least one other experienced and quality recruit from the Bronx. Three solid, experienced females will suffice.

Nine hours later, JaRew and I find ourselves with thousands of compatriots in search of what? We don't know. A reminder of the war between the people in a country designed by and for "we the people" to free some people.

The twilight and serene, almost collegial atmosphere comfort my spirit and quiet my emotions. If I am honest with myself, I have to admit that my feelings are hurt. Worse, I have to also admit that I no longer trust Beckham Johnson, something I would have never imagined. I'm embarrassed to share this fiasco with anyone. JaRew tried more than once this afternoon to discuss the situation, but I've refused. I know I will have to confront Beckham about it. If I don't, I'm no better than him. Even worse, if I don't, JaRew will take it to the source without a moment's hesitation. That's the last thing I need him to do. JaRew is not one to back away from anything. Neither am I, but I like to think things through. JaRew acts and then maybe thinks. He's not one to care about the consequences of his actions. His philosophy: he'd handle it.

Tired after the horrendous meeting and the long day of walking the Washington Mall, we sit a few yards below President Lincoln's feet. A whispered hush surrounds us, unlike the humble but nonstop chatter prevalent at the Martin Luther King, Jr. Memorial— our earlier stop. Jarewski and I share the last water bottle, periodically taking a swig of the lukewarm Fiji. *I wish I were in Fiji.* I take another sip before handing the almost empty bottle back to JaRew. I'm exhausted, and my brain churns as my stomach growls. "Hey, Blue Lady. You up for dinner?"

I rub my stomach as though to quiet its public service announcement.

"Sorry about that. I guess I am." I laugh. "Hey, any way we can call a cab?"

Walking two miles back to the car parked on a side street west of the White House is mind-boggling at this point.

"I think the city's resolved the Uber/Lyft issue, by the way."

"Oh, really?"

"Yep, they finally realized rules are rules." He added he was sorry those rules didn't include a pick up from our luxe seats from the top step of the monument.

I sigh again. Not sure at all how I feel sitting below the feet of the man who was on the side to free my ancestors.

As though he senses my ambiguous thoughts and the raging conflict in my spirit, I hear JaRew rambling on about historical facts and philosophies.

"So, are we drum majors for justice and peace, Ange? And do you think it's true that peace cannot be kept by force; it can only be achieved by understanding?" He sips from the Fiji bottle and passes it back to me.

"What about darkness? Was Dr. King right? Is it true that darkness cannot drive out darkness; only light can do that?"

My thoughts are as jumbled as an Italian Frittata—a spicy one with jalapeno peppers. I feel a distinct nudge from Blue Lady and whisper, "JaRew, I think we have to be the light driving out the darkness. I'm thinking this project is designed to help us understand what's behind the violence in New York. Revelation and knowledge can only come from understanding. Yes, Dr. King was right. We both know what the data shows." I guzzle the last of the Fiji. I'm embarrassed to realize I've been so busy focusing on the statistics, I've overlooked the true significance of the numbers.

"And I'm just beginning to correlate the numbers to reality. Every plus one translates to another depressed mother."

JaRew nods, continuing to stare across the Mall and adds, "Another generation of broken spirits."

The data Beckham shared in our last meeting and my own personal research of New York State, now the official target of our project blows my mind. I know the numbers speak for themselves. They're screaming from the charts! Thousands of people are dying! And many more are wounded. Guns are the enemy of the people. Or do I have it twisted? Hmmm. I check my thought process. We're our own worst enemy. People are the enemy of the people. Wow!

"You're awfully quiet over there."

"Sorry. Just thinking."

"About?"

"The numbers. The data. You know—the info Beckham and his sidekick shared on community violence."

"And?"

"How did you feel about them, Ange?"

I decide to go for it. "The numbers or the 'them'?"

We now face each other, still sitting at our sixteenth president's feet. Too tired to move. Too exhausted for me to share that I'm somewhat comforted by the surreal presence of President Lincoln.

"Don't know what you mean, Blue Lady." His normally piercing hazel eyes twinkle as he adds, "I knew it would be just a matter of time before she joined us."

I smile and shake my head. Me, too.

"Actually, I miss her." I'm surprised at his sentimental confession, and even more so by the touch of his hand on mine. Other than my best friend Nicole, JaRew is the only person who understands me and my alter ego. I shock myself by giggling. Yep, the Blue Lady has definitely shown her face making her presence known to me, JaRew, and the stoic Mr. Lincoln. I purse my lips, realizing I hadn't freshened my makeup since this morning. I unzip my Kate Spade powder blue crossbody bag and search around for my hot cinnamon Altoids.

I find it ironic that Beckham coined my Blue Lady nickname but doesn't know the real me. Not the other side of me. He couldn't know me—not after the sabotage today. The face I only share on rare occasions. I'm not surprised that Blue Lady showed up. I'm glad she didn't intervene on my behalf at the meeting. Now that I think of it, maybe she did. It's the numbers. *No, it's not*, Blue Lady argues. *It's your reaction to those numbers, Silly. Your emotions are leading this train—not your brain.*

MY EMOTIONS RUN DEEP—I've accepted that I hide them. Bury them. They make me weak. And I've learned when you plan to be the best, there's no room at the top for a sniffling woman. Hard decisions demand a hard heart. *Do they? You sure about that?* I ignore Blue Lady.

Numbers can talk. Analysis and number crunching are critical to defining the problem. Its scope. Its depth. And I've checked. There's enough consistency from source to source to know I'm looking at the facts—and not fly-by-night dramatized fake numbers.

Intellectually, the numbers make no sense to me. Eight deaths over eight days, and nobody knows anything about the why, the who? As I now focus for the first time on the truth behind the numbers, I identify the missing facts:

Numbers are people.

Numbers are someone's parents.

Numbers are someone's children.
Grandchildren.

Cousins. Sisters. Brothers. Aunts. Uncles.

I realize crunching more numbers is not the answer. Regional and within region data and comparisons are not the answer. Something's wrong. Deadly wrong. I can't explain it because I don't understand. And if I can't understand it, my MO says, get a handle on this—you'll be wasting your time if you don't.

"Do you understand this violence-in-the-street stuff, JaRew?" I turn because I search for truth in his eyes that rarely conceal anything, although they're quite capable of messaging what he wants them to. We've worked together long enough for me to be able to read him like a bestselling novel by one of my favorite authors. His deep-set hazel eyes are mirrors to his soul. "I don't. And I've worked the streets before, but this is different, Ange." I return his pain-filled gaze.

"I don't understand, and..."

"I know, cause if I don't..." He laughed.

"You can laugh. I admit I'm a sheltered bougie."

I examine my fresh manicure, frown, and sigh. How can I worry about a tiny nail chip—when as many as five black kids somewhere in our land of the free and home of the brave will die from a gunshot? Today. Most likely, right down the street from their front doors. My mind flips to one of the graphs that Cooke shared in our team meeting. Stats from last week. A small city in upstate New York. Albany, I think. Two cousins, sixteen and seventeen, were shot, bodies decimated by a .45 caliber handgun as they stood side by side outside a neighborhood convenience store eating sunflower seeds. Per their friends' reports, they didn't even have time to spit out their crushed shells. My voice cracks when I say, "JaRew?" He turns. I don't wait for a response.

"Maybe we do need Dez Cooke."

A never experienced part of me was ready to drop out of the project, collect my Georgia unemployment and put on my job search black pumps. JaRew was down with the idea, reminding me he could always find a black suit somewhere. I hadn't talked to Jocelyn, but I wanted to run this whole scenario by her. Besides, she knows how to get around in the Big Apple. If Cooke is right about new grant funding coming out of New York, we can get ahead of the game, put our feelers out, and check for ourselves. Definitely time to track down my contacts. I can write my own friggin' grant. It wouldn't be the first time.

"Hey, are you all right over there?"

"I'm good, JaRew." I decide to keep my thoughts to myself. I'm not one to back down from anything. Or anyone. But I'm more than capable of going after what I want. My head is spinning. Question: What do I want?

He wraps my hand in his. "Are you sure you want to do this?"

I don't respond, but privately admit, I really don't know.

CHAPTER THREE

"It's time for you to meet Mighty Man."

I'D FINISHED packing and was checking the dresser drawers for personal items when the phone rings. I expect to hear JL's cheery, "Ciao, Bella." Instead, a deep voice politely informs me I have a package at the concierge desk. Rather than wait until checkout, I decide to go down to pick it up, assuming it was an update from Beckham on the project.

The attendant quickly finds my package, has me sign for it, and wishes me a good day. Since I plan to use self-checkout, I tell the pleasant-looking young attendant that service has been excellent, and as usual, I have no complaints. He smiles and encourages me to complete the hotel's customer service satisfaction survey.

"Will do." I wink and head toward the elevator.

I push the up button at the elevator, shove the lighter-than-expected UPS box under my arm, and text JaRew, "See u at ten." I shake the box, feeling like a little kid whose parents have forbidden her to open an early Christmas present. I don't recognize the return address on the package. From habit, I double-bolt the door, moving quickly to the desk drawer to find something to help me open the triple-cellophane taped box. I shake the box again, wondering what it could be. Who knows where I am? Out of the blue, my heart pounds as I think of the truer than true stories of people poisoned when opening specially delivered boxes. My hands tremble, and the box falls to the floor with no help from my non-functioning fingers.

I scream at the louder-than-loud pounding at the door. I back farther away from the box, afraid to walk past it to open the door.

"Hey! Angelica! Open the door! It's me. JaRew. Open up!"

The pounding continues. My legs go on strike.

"Are you all right in there?"

I creep over to the door, alarmed, and peer through the peephole despite the familiarity of the voice. I slide the lock and turn the handle. "What the hell is going on?" All I want to do is sit.

I tiptoe around the still unopened box and collapse onto the side chair—the one farthest from the mystery package.

I close the drapes as Jarewski shuts the door. I hear the lock.

"What are you doing?"

As he walks toward me, he sees the box and bends to pick it up.

"Don't!"

"Don't what?"

"Don't touch that box!"

"Don't touch it? What's in it?" What the heck is wrong with me?

"Well, well, well. Isn't this interesting?" I hear plastic rustling.

I open my eyes. JaRew holds up two small boxes, walks over, and hands me a slip of paper.

"Call me ASAP. We need to go over a few things. Use these burners. They're charged. Btw, we need to keep our convos under the radar.

-- Dez, aka the Mighty Man."

I pass the note back to JaRew.

"Just who does this guy think he is? Mighty Man? Is he for real?" I shake my head in disbelief. I don't know which is worse—Cooke's ridiculous message or my equally ridiculous behavior. I realize I don't want to deal with either.

"Have you heard from Beckham, Ange? I thought you were running the show. What's going on?" Good question. Don't ask me.

As though reading my mind, he adds, "Don't you think it's time you found out?"

I ball up the note and slam it toward the wastebasket. It bounces off the edge and lands four inches short.

JaRew picks it up and easily tosses it in. I groan in self-defeat and realize it's decision time.

I grab my iPhone and see that I have no missed phone calls other than two from JaRew.

"So, what's going on, Blue Lady?"

"Not a darn thing. Chuck those phones, JaRew." Mighty Man... Humph. Enough is enough. "And leave Blue Lady out of this! You're right on one thing, though. Who does Cooke think he is?"

More importantly, who does Beckham think he is?

I'm nobody's soft touch.

Of course, Blue Lady decides to remind me of a few things. *You're gonna have to shove those emotions aside, Angelica. If you don't, you'll never make it through this project, Ms. Fix the World. You better learn to stand your ground, Girl!*

JaRew's ringtone interrupts the private exchange between Blue Lady and me.

"What do you want, Cooke?" He hits the speaker button. I give him a thumbs-up.

"You and Angelica, chuck those fancy BS iPhones. Stop being jerks! Going forward, use the ones I sent. Got it?"

"Cooke, I don't know where you get off, but I don't take my orders from you."

"You want to bet your check on it?"

Losing it, I snatch the phone. "You want to bet your job?"

"You might want to touch base with the man, Ms. Mason." Cooke's haughty laugh makes me sick to my stomach. JaRew moves as if to take the phone. I shake my head. This is my battle.

Click! I hit the red circle on JaRew's phone.

Cooke may know the streets. But I can learn the streets.

He may *think* he knows Beckham. I *know* that I know Beckham.

Before hitting the road, JaRew and I stop by Walmart. Two new phones, it is.

CHAPTER FOUR

"Did you watch the local news last night?"

WE'RE ON OUR WAY to pick up JL from the airport. She's flying in from NYC. We haven't briefed her on the project yet, but she was shocked when I told her about Beckham's turncoat shenanigans. We plan to fill her in today. But I figure he's still the boss—for now, anyway. I think about the paycheck I should receive shortly and smile at the motivation it provides. I can deal with Beckham *and* his Dez Cooke.

Mr. Johnson or BJ, as Cooke calls him, may have forgotten. I make it a point to win at whatever I do. I admit I'm frightened by the thought of exposing myself to street-level violence, but I'm a fighter—not physically, but I always aim to make a difference—regardless of where I find myself. The obstacles I've faced in the past have not been bullets, but I've hurdled some brick walls.

I learned a long time ago that sometimes you have to do what you have to do to get where you want to go.

And I want to run this project. Although it's not what I expected, I'll find a way to work it. Or find something bigger and better.

Jarewski hasn't said a word on the drive down, which means he's planning and scheming. He tunes in to the local jazz station. I don't know how he feels about my inviting Jocelyn to join us. I didn't ask, and he didn't react when I shared my plan. Not a surprise. JaRew is smooth as silk and is more than capable of taking on a million different roles. I call him my lean, clean chameleon. I know to expect the unexpected.

He'll let me know when he's firmed up his thoughts.

"Did you watch the local news last night?" JaRew adjusts the volume.

Upon arrival last night, we checked into a local hotel in Scotia, a cute little suburb not too far from

Blue Lady's MISSION under FIRE

Albany. We plan to transition to our home away from home later today. We'd reserved a three-bedroom Airbnb in Ballston Lake away from the center of the action, so we assume. Only time will tell. Per the rental description, the small cottage is tucked away on a quarter of an acre of farmland and not visible from any major road or highway. It has its own pond, been recently remodeled, but has been vacant for years. A young, newly married couple inherited the property from the wife's grandfather. According to the rental manager, it's a new listing. It seems to perfectly meet our needs and is about an hour or so from downtown Albany. No one knows about our hideaway.

Not Beckham. Not my father. And certainly not Cooke. "No. By the way, I'm sorry about the phone incident, JaRew. I don't know what happened. I guess I lost it for a moment there."

"Yeah, I think you did."

We chuckle, both deciding to let sleeping dogs lie, as the expression goes. Dez Cooke isn't going anywhere anytime soon, and to develop my plan, I need to be proactive and anticipate his next move.

"I plan to call Beckham once you, JL, and I chat."

JaRew doesn't respond, which is his way of saying, "I hear you."

We continue our drive to the smooth rhythm of Brian Culbertson. JaRew enters the New York State Thruway, the quickest route to the airport.

"Oh, sorry. No. Local—wait; actually, all news was off the table for me last night. I opted to read the speech that Beckham gave last year at the National Mayor's Conference. He told me that the Conference supported his bid for the STV funding. Yeah, he thinks that move may have been a game-changer. I thought the speech might provide insight into Beckham's overall thinking on the project."

"Did it?"

"Not really, but it contained some useful background information."

I glance over and ask, "Why? The news, I mean?"

"Five people were killed this past weekend in Albany. The annual Tulip Festival."

"You're kidding me, right?" He turns, delivering a frown that messages, "C'mon now, Ange. Don't you get it?"

"I know. I know. Figure of speech, okay?" I shake my head. "I guess I'm shocked," I mumble. "Those two teenagers were shot a few days before we arrived and—"

"Hey, Boss Lady! I got news for you. This is our new way of life ! Have you forgotten why we're here?"

JaRew's over-the-top response doesn't require an answer. He's frustrated, too. I'm sure the project design doesn't bother him, but I'm positive that he's upset about Beckham's treatment of me. And I also know he and Cooke won't get along. Not at all. They're like a defective homemade bomb. I again wonder about Beckham's about-face on the personnel side of the revised plan. I make a mental note to reevaluate my initial thinking before I call him.

"I know. I know. I just feel so bad for the people. The families. The neighborhoods." I ignore the lump in my throat.

"Facts."

"Facts?"

"Yeah, if we're taking this project on, Ange, we have to face our new reality, don't you think?"

"Yeah, I guess." My runaway thoughts escape with no warning. "Do you want to know what I'm really thinking?"

This time he turns to stare at me long enough for me to remind him: "Hey, you're driving!"

The driver blasts his horn and gives JaRew the bird as he swerves to the left and around us.

JaRew reciprocates with a hard lean on the Escape's horn but stops short of flipping his middle finger. He grins instead as though the irate driver can see him through his rearview mirror.

We both laugh—glad at the opportunity to be able to experience some of life's silliness.

"Now tell me, Ange. Just what are you thinking?"

"Forget it for now. Let's discuss it later with JL." It's too soon for me to be tired of thinking, but I am.

"Not a problem."

Blue Lady's MISSION under FIRE

We exit from I-87 South, following the signs for the airport. My phone chirps.

JL's text reads: "Just landed."

JL AND I haven't seen each other since I took my leave of absence from my Smoothville, Georgia city manager position to help my mother take care of my dad during his recovery. He'd really scared us with his heart attack. Normally a healthy man, his attack frightened him, too. Not that he'd ever admit it. But thankfully, he's doing much better and assures me he's maintaining the new dietary routine—no fried chicken. He's also joined one of the local gyms.

Jocelyn is hanging onto her deputy mayor position by a thread. Luke Evans had violated every promise he made to her when he convinced her to become his deputy. She lost the last mayoral race to him, then incumbent, by a small margin. She'd begun plans to seek a re-count when Luke offered to make her one of his deputies and give her oversight responsibility of a to-be-established grassroots community council. She licked her wounds, camouflaged her psychological bruises, and trusted him. JL wants me to lead her planned face-off with him in the next election. I haven't decided yet. I'm tempted after the way he's treated JaRew and me. I just don't know if revenge should be my motivation, however.

JaRew packed up his desk and walked out the front door of Smoothville City Hall without a word when he learned that Luke was not only scheming to fire me but was also planning to replace me with my ex-boyfriend and high school sweetheart, Shawn Mallory. With a little arm twisting, I convinced him to work with me on the STV project.

Needless to say, the three of us have a lot to talk about.

I stand up and wave to JL as she exits the terminal. She smiles and quickens her pace. JaRew had dropped me off at the baggage claims area while he circled the terminal to avoid paying the one-hour parking fee. He never fails to amaze me. Fifteen dollars was too much to spend for a parking space, but he'd spend a hundred dollars on a bottle of wine.

Blue Lady's MISSION under FIRE

Jocelyn looks good. With a lot of help from the summer sun, her naturally curly hair had blondish streaks. The free-spirited ringlets bounced in rhythm with her sassy, hip-swinging, long strides. When teased about her saucy trot, she'd wink and argue, "What can you do when nature blesses you with a tush?"

"Hey, JL!"

"Hey, Chica. ¿Qué pasa? Where's JaRew?"

CHAPTER FIVE

"Hey! Let's check out the territory."

"I'M STUFFED. Whose great idea was this?" Jocelyn and I both point at Jarewski, who ignores us as he tackles the last of his New York-style cheesecake.

I also notice for the first time that he's growing a beard. "JaRew, not getting personal or anything, but did you forget to shave this morning?" I chuckle in appreciation of my own joke. "Don't tell me you're trying to sport a beard?"

"Nice job, Ange. Just like you're working with the lingo, I'm developing the look. Besides, I've always wanted a beard. The time—or should I say, the setting —never seemed right. A political consulting firm, then a small-town mayor's office in the deep south—never seemed right, you know?"

"And now, what are ya?"

He munches. "I don't know yet. Tryin' to get a feel for it."

He wipes his mouth with the back of his hand.

"JaRew!"

"Just saying. What's it look like? Should I carry my lily-white cloth napkin when I go to the hood?"

Taking advantage of his role-play, he scoops a big hunk of cheesecake with his spoon and gobbles away.

"JaRew, you're disgusting."

"So you say. This is the best cheesecake I've ever had."

"And what does that have to do with your manners or lack thereof?" Jocelyn shakes her head and frowns. "Living in the inner city doesn't mean you don't have manners. Did you forget I'm from the Bronx?"

JaRew ignores her. I encourage his shenanigans with my best imitation of a sassy wink.

He fist-bumps me.

JL shakes her head and frowns.

"Don't mind us, JL, we're practicing. JaRew says I'm too bougie." I grin. "Besides, New York Style cheesecake is his favorite dessert."

She peers at me. "Si, he's right. We need to do some shopping, Chica.

"I noticed the beard, too, Jarewski, but decided it was none of my business. But what's going on between you two? What have I missed?" She twists in her chair to face JaRew, peering at him as though he was someone she'd just met. I ignore the comment, not quite knowing what to make of it. When neither of us responds, JL shrugs her shoulders and continues as if she never asked the question.

"Well, thanks again for picking me up from the airport. What are we doing this afternoon, by the way?" JL and JaRew have had their ups and downs, depending on the day of the week. This tripartite arrangement should be interesting if nothing else.

"It's time to split. Let's check out the territory." JaRew looks at his watch and nods at me. I agree. The dinner crowd will be arriving in the next couple of hours. We've been here much too long. Too loud.

Blue Lady's MISSION under FIRE

And too comfortable. In one of the most popular venues in the town. In the middle of one of the area's two biggest malls. Some undercover team. I'm sure Cooke would have some choice words for us.

I don't share that Beckham called during lunch. My "ritzy" iPhone shows a message, but I'm not falling for that trick. For all I know, Cooke's told him about my refusal to use his Mighty Man phones, and I don't want to have that discussion. Until JL, Jarewski, and I work out our own game plan, Mr. Johnson can sit and wait. When we work out the details of our plan within a planned strategy, I'll reach out to Beckham. I don't need a plan to decide whether I interact with Cooke.

I'm not.

FOR NOW, we plan to scout the city. Separately.

JaRew's taking the city bus. It runs all day, six days a week. And this is prime time. People have begun their commute home. He plans to ride it from the small town right outside of Albany to downtown Schenectady. He'll then make the return trip and ride to downtown Albany where we plan to meet up at the city's summer music fest held at the Hudson River waterfront.

I'm driving the rental. I plan to cruise around the city to get a feel for the local businesses.

JL plans to check out the mall and local shops and the vibe of the shoppers. Uber is the word for her.

We plan to meet up around six-thirty. The Alive at Five music event starts at five. We'll see how easily we blend into the crowd when we arrive.

THE RIDE down and around town doesn't take as long as I expect, even driving down Central Avenue, Albany's version of Main Street, USA. The drive is pleasant enough to not be worried about an irate driver pulling into your lane without warning, unlike metro ATL. Local speed limits are capped at 35 or 40 mph. While travel is steady, there are only a few pedestrians, most waiting for a bus. Quite different from NYC or Hot-Lanta, where throngs of sightseers are a rule of thumb.

As I near the center of the city, Kroger and Publix of Georgia are replaced by Hannaford and Price

Blue Lady's MISSION under FIRE

Chopper. An abundance of community-owned shops, including neighborhood all-purpose food and supply shops, aren't at all intimidated by the chain store competition. Specialty pizza, fried chicken and sub shops, beauty shops, and "pick up your locally made brews" marts compete with each other for business. I conclude that Albany has its share of imbibers evidenced by the two or three liquor stores within each city block. I smile as I realize some things don't change from city to city or state to state.

Street parking is allowed. Most spots are taken.

After driving a few more blocks, I notice the change in pedestrian attire. Low-hanging jeans, hip-hugging denim shorts, bright, graphic tees, and halter tops have been replaced with business casual: dark suits and low-heeled pumps. Historically designated buildings house professional law offices replacing the three-story brick buildings in the previous blocks.

Main Street, USA, marks the official border between businesses and residential areas. I learn later in my sightseeing tour that a sharp left or right at almost any major intersection provides the entrance to a possible world of no return.

Traffic picks up. I hope the huge digital grandfather clock on the colossal brick church tower is wrong. A quick glance at my watch confirms the clock is right. I'm definitely running behind schedule. I only have an hour and a half before my meetup with JL and JaRew. My leisurely tour of the city is just about done. On a whim, I turn on the radio. Local music is always a good way to pick up a city's vibe. I quickly turn it off, deciding I can't allow the music to distract me from my visual map.

Three city blocks later, I find myself surrounded by office buildings that house small delis and newsstands. I've obviously entered the work zone of New York

State's civil servants and legislative staffers. The pace is even quicker in the blocks leading to the official center of government. City Hall's flag waves a welcome to me as I wait at the longer-than-normal stoplight. A quick glance at my GPS confirms that I'm right and that the state legislative office building is to my immediate right, making the state capitol the majestic-looking building on the right in the next block. I think it would be nice if I catch a glimpse of NYS Governor Cuomo leaving the building. I watch his brother, Chris Cuomo on CNN's prime time news slot every night. JL thinks Andrew has a long way to go if he plans to come even close to attaining equal status with his father, one of the best ever New York State governors—or so she claims.

Governor Andrew recently announced the state's plans to honor his father with a walking and bike path over the Governor Mario M. Cuomo Bridge. The previously named Tappan Zee Bridge is being revamped to include a walking and biking path that will include six themed overlooks for cyclists and pedestrians. Without more than a ten-second trip down wishful thinking lane, I dismiss my idea of making a weekend trip to New York City. Theatre, shopping, and people watching don't mesh well with my undercover lifestyle.

I'm soon reminded I have to second-guess my GPS after turning down a short one-way street. Short enough for me to be more than halfway down it before I realize that I'm heading in the wrong direction. And fortunate enough for me, the street is ghosted. My new vocabulary is growing on me. JaRew would be proud of me.

Deciding I'd better avoid the late-afternoon work traffic and pedestrians, I make two rights and find myself driving back up Central Avenue, heading in the direction I'd just left. I don't have time to be going in circles. I pick up my pace. I'm on Lark Street, a street that is mentioned in one of the city guides. I make a mental note to revisit the area. The eclectic array of shops, restaurants, tattoo parlors, and strollers present a vibe different from those I'd already experienced in my short afternoon cruise through the city. Interesting.

I make another left. Traffic slows but is too heavy to allow for serious sightseeing. Hmmm, Bombers. Now that's different. Might have to check that out — Café Hollywood. I chuckle. A Hollywood café mid-city upstate New York. Two blocks down, a huge Washington Park sign welcomes me. Periodic quick glances to my left and right suffice for now — sufficient detail to share with JaRew and JL to help us map out the next steps. An irate driver leans on his car horn. Okay, already! I dismiss my urge to return the honk. I pick up my pace. Next stop.

CHAPTER SIX

"Can you take me to Daddy's spot, please?"

A LAUNDROMAT. I can't remember the last time I saw one. I hear JaRew's rejoinder. "You come from a different world, Boss Lady." I don't even try to refute it anymore. He's right.

"SOS, we serve the best." The unique front window of the tiny eat-in, takeout restaurant catches my attention, but my heart quickens at the huge, larger-than life black, red, and green RIP mural on the building next to it. It's beautiful. A part of me wants to pull over and take a picture. The power of the billboard-sized weaponry superimposed over a small peaceful community surrounded by tombstones makes me question my attraction to the image. As I reflect on this, I realize my desire to savor the image is my involuntary reaction to the beauty of the artwork. It serves its intended purpose. The message is crystal clear.

"Yo, will you move it, lady? You're holdin' up traffic!"

At first, I think the driver is speaking to me. Another impatient driver on the opposite side of the road blasts his car horn and turns up his sound system.

My heart tugs when I see the cutest little boy struggling to keep up with his mother as she lugs her laundry bag on one shoulder with his sister on her hip. I sigh and think, Bless his little heart. He's doing his share. His bright blue NY Yankees cap is much too big for him and falls off his head as he struggles with a miniature wheeled laundry cart.

The little boy's eyes widen as he scoots in front of his mother. Socks, underwear, and a T-shirt fall from the laundry bag that topples over in his cart. His mother quickens her pace as the driver guns his motor. The driver pulls around me. His dated but buffed black Mercedes rolls over the little boy's hat. Tears stream down the child's face as he points to his now crumpled cap.

I pull over at the next available spot, park the Escape, grab my keys, and hop out. The Yankees cap is bantered back and forth as the passing vehicles play ping pong with it. I jog down the sidewalk, following the cap, waiting for the traffic light to turn red. I lose sight of it when a black pickup trunk flattens it. I groan but continue my trek. Finally, as the truck pulls off, I see that the cap is lodged against the curb on the opposite side of the road. I backtrack, and once the light changes, I cross the street and pick up the hat, hoping it can withstand a much-needed tumble in the washer. Regardless, it's still wearable, but beat-up for sure. I trot back to the laundry. My little friend sees me from the laundromat window and smiles when he realizes I have his prized possession.

His mother opens the door for me. Baby Girl has slept through all the drama. Her head is settled comfortably against her mother's chest.

"Hey, little man. Does this belong to you?" He smiles and nods his head, wiping his tears with one hand and snatching his hat with the other.

"Honey, don't be rude. Tell the lady 'thank you.'"

"Thank you, miss."

For the first time, I see that little man's mother can't be more than twenty. "You're welcome. May I put your hat on your head, or do you want your mommy to wash it first?"

Little man nods and points to his head.

"You sure? I'm sorry it got so dirty." I look to his mother for her okay. She nods.

"Say thank you, Jaylen."

"Thank you." He reaches for his mother's hand.

"You have a good day, Jaylen."

Jaylen rewards me with a huge grin.

His mother thanks me again. And again. Before I can tell her I really didn't do anything, little Jaylen whispers, "Mommy, can we go to Daddy's spot? Maybe the lady can take us."

I look at my watch. I have less than thirty minutes to meet up with JaRew and JL. And I don't have a clue how far I am from the waterfront.

"Honey, the lady can't take us. We have to wash clothes, and she doesn't have the time. She's busy."

She nods and winks at me as though to say, "Don't worry. We're okay."

"But, Mommy—"

"Shhh, honey. I told you no." The baby stirs. Her mother pats her back. I feel so sorry for the young mom. I wonder how she's able to wash clothes with a baby on her hip, a whimpering child at her knee, and a missing-in-action husband. I become angry thinking about how women are so challenged by the struggles of day-to-day life. Her husband could have at least watched the kids while she was at the laundry. I chide myself when I realize how quickly I've judged a man I don't even know.

"But, Mommy, I want to show Daddy my hat!" He takes off the cap and rubs it with his hand in an effort to remove the grime.

"He bought me this hat just before that gun shot him. Remember, Mommy? He told me he'd help me keep it clean. So, we could be like twins. I promised to keep my hat clean like his." He begins to cry. "And that car dirtied up my Yankee hat, Mommy. Will Daddy be mad at me?"

He stomps his foot. "I have to go see Daddy, Mommy. I have to tell him. It's not my fault. Please, Mommy."

The baby screams. Jaylen's mom bursts into tears. "Your daddy ain't mad at you, Jaylen. He's dead! I told you he's dead."

OMG. I'm bawling. Does she really mean *dead*?

What does a five or six-year-old know about death?

Little Jaylen harmonizes with Baby Girl—the two of them crying the blues. Baby Girl just stares at me with huge crocodile-like tears running down her face.

The other customers shake their heads. Some whisper. Some appear concerned. Others are frustrated. Someone yells out to the laundromat attendant, "Hey, can you give us some volume on the TV? I can't hear it over these screeching kids."

"Yeah, could you please?" Another customer chimes in. "Should be a law. No kids under twelve in the laundromat."

"I know what you mean. My favorite soap is on." I look at my watch—twenty-five minutes. I sigh.

"Miss, can I give you a ride somewhere?"

I hear my phone beep. Oh, no! They're looking for me!

The young mother panics. Her laundry baskets are shoved to the side. Someone had moved them from the entrance to the door. Baby Girl is happily slurping on her bottle. Little man sucks his thumb, holding his hat close to his chest.

"Can I give you a ride, ma'am? It looks like you're not going to be able to wash today. Why don't I take you home?" JaRew's going to want to kill me, but I forge ahead, taking a quick look at my watch. "Want to go for a ride, buddy?"

"My name is Jaylen. Did you hear my mommy? She keeps telling me Daddy's dead. She says he's not coming back. I got to tell him I'm sorry about my hat. I don't want him to be mad at me. Can you take me to Daddy's spot? Please?"

JaRew is down at the waterfront. He texts that I should plan to have problems finding a parking space.

I respond: "Mini-emergency; don't worry. Explain later."

He responds. "Prk under bridge--on grass."

"OK, thx!"

RASHIDA DIRECTS me down the streets of Albany's west end. With a fuller picture of her story, I feel guilty about my prior judgments and marvel at her coping, do-what-I-have-to-do lifestyle. I now have so much respect for the man I never knew but who had been strong enough to teach his son so much in their short time together.

Little man knows how to love. He knows respect.

Character traits many adults don't possess.

In just about an hour, Jaylen has reminded me of the importance of trust. He trusts me. And more importantly, the significance of the biblical admonition, "Judge not lest ye be judged." I've never considered myself to be judgmental. Today, I realize I have a lot of work to do. Images of my ex-boss, Luke; my new boss, Beckham; and recently ordained, co-team leader, Desmond Cooke flitter through my mind.

Blue Lady's MISSION under FIRE

My eyes widen as I realize how much I've judged my mother for how little she did to help me when I took my leave of absence to help her care for my father after his heart attack last year.

Suddenly aware of the sound of the silence, I see that Baby Girl is still asleep, protected by Rashida's arms and the seat belt. Jaylen, my little man, quietly sucks his thumb in the back seat. His mother sits stiff as a board, staring straight ahead. I had ignored her objections that they could walk home. "The same way we came," she'd argued. I assured her that I had no problem taking them to the "spot" as Jaylen called it. When I add that I'd wait for them and drop them off at home, she doesn't bother to hide the escaping tears. I hand her a tissue and hold her hand for a couple of seconds. It's cold as ice.

I no longer know what to say, and rather than try to make small talk, I say nothing. Anything I might say at this point would be meaningless in the overall scheme of things. I'm sure one more "I'm sorry for your loss" will do nothing to improve the emptiness she must feel.

Music has its way of making me feel better, so I ask, "Do you want to listen to the radio?"

She shakes her head and continues to pat Baby Girl. I've never had to think about child seat belt laws —never had a reason to think of them, but she had and points out that she only lives a few blocks away, and she'll pray that we don't get stopped by a policeman.

I decide to rely on her prayer and cross my fingers

to be on the extra-safe side. The last thing I need is to get pulled over. Let's go for it.

"I'm so tired," she mumbles under her breath but doesn't respond to my well-intended but somewhat meaningless, "I'm sorry."

She sighs. "Turn after this light. Sorry, right turn, please."

I wait for the light and peek through my rearview mirror at Little Man. His eyes are squeezed tight as though he's fighting something.

"The light's green."

"Oops, thank you, Rashida. Take the next right?"

"Yes, Manning Avenue. Drive to the first corner. You can park on the right, but it's on the left."

I don't know what "it" is and prepare myself for the worst. I slow, nervous about all the little kids playing on the sidewalk. It looks as though the neighbors are having a block party. Portable grills are spaced intermittently from house to house. Stevie Wonder's "I Just Called to Say I Love You" makes my heart hurt for Little Man and his mother. The smell of spicy barbecue sauce causes my stomach to grumble. The succulent aroma makes me wonder if the neighbors are cooking chicken or ribs or both.

"There it is, Miss. Miss. Miss…? Do you see it?"

I smile. "Angelica, Jaylen. My name is Angelica."

"There it is, Miss Angel. Daddy's angel looks just like you, Miss Angel. Doesn't she, Mommy?"

As she loosens the seat belt, Rashida turns to look at me. Her eyes speak sadness; her tone, heartfelt gratitude.

"Yes, honey. Ms. Angelica does look like Daddy's angel. C'mon, Jaylen, let's go say hi to Daddy so we can get home before dark."

"I'll wait for you. I can drive you home."

"You don't need to be around here after seven, Angelica. The demons come out. This is a dark, dark place."

"But..."

She shuts the door, quickly turning to help little Jaylen. He hops out, pointing down the street.

I open the truck to get Rashida's laundry. "I can take that, ma'am."

The darkest of dark sunglasses conceal the eyes of the well-dressed man who towers over me. Caught off guard, I step back.

"Hey there, Jaylen."

"Hi, Reverend Bahari. This is Ms. Angel. She brought us home so we can go to Daddy's spot. Doesn't she look like Daddy's angel?"

The man removes his glasses. His deep, brown-black eyes smile. "I think she does, Jay. How are you, Miss? I'm Reverend Shabazz—Bahari Shabazz." He shakes my hand and then quickly pats Jaylen on the head. "Hey, what happened to your hat, Buddy?"

Jaylen takes his hand, and they walk off side by side. The minister removes Jaylen's cap and brushes it against his slacks in an effort to remove some of the mud. Jaylen pulls his laundry cart behind him. Rashida waves as she follows.

My phone beeps as I slide into the car. I don't need to look to know the sender.

Google helps me out.

"On my way. Where are you?"

"Down by the river. Are you okay?"

"I'm okay. See you soon."

I lie. I'm anything but "okay." I slow to a creep as I approach the corner left side of the street. A group of people have gathered and are kneeling to light candles. Jaylen kneels. Reverend Shabazz helps him light his candle.

CHAPTER SEVEN

"Ain't no half-Steppin'…"

FIVE ALIVE IS INDEED ALIVE. JaRew was right. I circle a few times before finding a spot under the bridge. I'm squeezed between two black SUVs—a Lexus and a Rogue—on a grassy slope. I dismiss my concern about a possible dent to the rental, figuring I'll deal with it when or if it happens. JaRew and I have exchanged multiple text messages. It seems like we both have a lot to share. JL is stranded somewhere between Schenectady and Albany. The bus she was on had a flat, and the driver is waiting for a replacement bus. She's prepared to find somewhere to hang out and wait for me to pick her up after the concert.

I follow the music and find myself in the middle of other latecomers who seem to have timed their arrival to the special guest performer, Big Daddy Kane, a well-known rapper from the 80s. It sounds like the show is about to start. The crowd's energy is contagious. My pace picks up as I follow the other late arrivers. Some concert-goers actually jog past me as we hear the local DJ begin his introduction of the special guest. I kick in my power walk when I recognize the beats of "Ain't No Half-Steppin'," and I grin as I wonder what my dad would think if he knew I was at a Big Daddy Kane concert. Knowing him, he'd ask, "Why didn't you invite me?"

I decide to send him a few pics. He'd never forgive me if he later finds out that I had the opportunity to do so and didn't. If they're selling posters or other paraphernalia, I decide to get him something special. I love outdoor music concerts, and while I know the crowd will be elbow to elbow at the bottom of the stage, I'll make my way to the front, inch by inch. I break into a trot myself now as I get excited about my plan to send my daddy a pic of Big Daddy!

The stage is to my left, and as I enter the waterfront venue, I see that I have my work cut out for me. How the heck am I gonna wiggle my way through this crowd?

Hundreds of people are already crammed shoulder to shoulder in the roped-off breathing-room-only space below the front stage. With the ninety-degree temperatures, I think about ditching my photo shoot, and instead, just get Dad a souvenir.

Stagehands have cleared the stage, and the crowd roars, "Kane! Kane! Kane!

"Yo! Yo! Yo!"

"DJ G8 is in the buildin'! And y'all know if I'm good, so are all of ya! I'm not gonna hold y'all up, I'm not gonna drag it out, cause we are all here waiting to see the great, the legendary, the no half stepper—Big Daddy—Big Daddy Kane!"

So much for my decision. Ain't no half-steppin' here. I make my first step toward the stage.

CHAPTER EIGHT

"What kind of undercover agents are we?"

"WE NEED to watch for Jude Hinckley," I say.

"So, you saw him last night?"

"I did. Do you think it's a coincidence that we ended up in the same place?"

"I have a more important question. Is he tracking us? And if so, why?"

I sip my coffee and jot a note.

"Thanks for making breakfast, JL." I turn to JaRew. "Do you think Cooke's in town, too?"

"No problem regarding breakfast. Glad to do it. I'm glad you left the instructions for getting onto the property. The Uber driver left his lights—"

"Oh, no!" I groan and bang my forehead with my hand. "Dumb, dumb, dumb. What kind of undercover operatives are we?"

We look at each other and shake our heads. Words aren't necessary.

"We're definitely joining the conference call tonight.

It'll be interesting to see what Jude says. And scratch the plan to discuss our next moves after tonight's call. We need to do it ASAP. Like, now. Presuming you two haven't made other plans."

JaRew looks at JL. "If we have, we need to cancel them." He states the obvious. "We might need to relocate. Without waiting for confirmation, can you take that on, JL?"

I write JL next to "we have to move"—now the number one item on my list.

She doesn't balk at the assignment, but asks, "Who's Jude?"

JaRew gives the rundown on the Beckham/Cooke undercover street team concept, its plan to scout out Albany for answers to the recent outbreak of community shootings, and the decision that JaRew and I had made after Cooke's command that we use his Mighty Man burner phones. I fully brief JL on the last-minute change in funding, project goals, and the requirement that all funded projects have a street team in their selected target community.

Due to the breakdown in communication between Beckham and me, I share that we haven't connected with other team members, so we don't know what assignments have been given, if any, other than the bare bone outline discussed in our last meeting in DC. Cooke's directions were to "scout your territory."

"I figure we're on point." JaRew's smug expression and arched eyebrow suggest we might be on a different page, albeit the same playbook.

Tonight's conference call is intended to move the project forward. Everyone's expected to report in on their progress. We explain to JL that JaRew and I are the only team members authorized to work together. Other than that, street team members ignore each other in the field.

"So, you guys saw this Jude Hinkley last night at the concert?"

"Yes, ma'am," I answer as I add another action item to my growing list.

JaRew responds without looking up. "Ma'am?" He clears his throat and groans. "You're not a Southern belle anymore, Ange. Please. We have to be careful."

"You're right. I'm sorry." I know he's upset about the silly mistake with the Uber driver. We've got to tighten it up. I needlessly write, "tighten it up" on my notepad.

"And I don't believe in coincidences."

"Neither do I."

"Excuse me. What are you guys saying?" I ask the question, needing to clear the air to make sure we're on the same page.

They alternate with staccato responses.

"Hinkley was at Five Alive."

"So maybe he's really into rap music?" JL snickers.

"Yeah, right. He looks like it." We all laugh.

"Seriously, though. Do you think he saw us?"

JaRew doesn't bother to look my way. "Not a doubt."

JL and I don't question the basis for JaRew's conclusion. If JaRew and I both independently spotted him in the crowd, he definitely saw us. Oh, God...I'm failing the street team leader test. Badly.

JL looks at me. "What do you think?"

"He looked a hot mess." I laugh and add, "I'm liking this urban stuff."

JaRew looks up. "You're kidding me?"

"About the urban—"

"Nah, it's growing on you. I meant Jude. He looked all right. To me."

I screech, "C'mon, JaRew, wasn't he wearing that crazy purple tie?"

As though not to be outdone, JL asks, "And anyway, who wears a tie to an outdoor music concert?" JL and I giggle.

"Actually, his tie was hot pink, JaRew. It hung loosely around his collar. The knot hit him center chest. His shirt hung low to his hips." As an afterthought, I add, "Maybe he really does like the rapper. Big Daddy had on a pink tie, too."

"Maybe that's his version of street life." JL sips her coffee and laughs.

"Not the Jude we met, right, JaRew?" He nods his head and adds, "We definitely need to touch base with your boy, Cooke."

"He's not my boy," I snap before I realize it.

They both look up.

"Sorry. But you know we never trusted Jude. Cooke might even have him tracking us."

"True dat." JaRew offers up with a smirk.

I sip my lukewarm coffee and ignore his playful jab.

"Agree, but you think this Cooke will fess up to tonight on the call?" JL continues her struggle to explain away the gaping holes in our 1000-piece community project jigsaw puzzle.

"No, I don't, but he might let something slip. Besides, we need to touch base with him. No reason to give him any reason to think we're operating out of the norm. He already knows we chucked the phones. Actually, maybe you should check in with Mr. Johnson." JaRew doesn't bother to look at me. Nor do I bother to answer. I know he's right on all accounts. And he knows that I know that.

We didn't need to worry about the call. Our cell phones don't ring at midnight. Was the conference call canceled?

CHAPTER NINE

"Am I too young to die?"

AM I TOO young to die?

"NO! I'm not." I stifle my scream, remind myself to focus on my driving, and try to calm my racing heartbeat.

Blue Lady pokes me with a vengeance. *Are you talking to me?*

The nudge dares me to continue talking to her— my friend, the Blue Lady. She's indeed my best friend—my alter ego. I finally shared my innermost secret with Nicole, my BFF from college, my dad, and JaRew after years of struggling to conceal my personality quirk. At times like this, I know she's the one person I can trust.

She's my confidant: me—the other side of me.

My brain scrambles to make sense of the craziness around me. Why should an innocent, sweet child have to face the reality of losing his father through an act of violence that took place a block or so from his home?

How will little Jaylen ever feel safe? Blue Lady's not so-polite punch to my gut tells the truth that I already know by my verbal response to my internal questioning. "Am I too young to die?" The honest to God answer is no.

I tremble at the stark reality of my conclusion. Statistics don't lie. I'm thirty-two, well within the age group that seems to be the moving target for erratic, unpredictable game players and gunslingers in small cities across the country.

Hey, Lady.

I'm thankful for the mellow voice that interrupts my racing thoughts.

It's going to be all right.

I turn over, relieved that I have a few more hours to sleep. Blue Lady assures me, *we're going to be all right.*

CHAPTER TEN

"Excuse me, officer, but why did you pull me over?"

"I'M HERE. WHR R U?"

I groan, so glad she doesn't know just how far away I am. Like, forty-five minutes that don't include the time I need to park and find her. Before I can ask Google to respond to my new friend's "Whr r u?" JaRew's "So whr r u?" text pops up on the Ford's screen.

I wish for a two-for-one, hands-free texting system.

I decide to let them both wait.

The slam of the front door had announced JaRew's early morning departure. A one-eyed peek at my cell that shared my comfy down pillow had confirmed that it was indeed early. Six a.m. Much too early for me.

Blue Lady's MISSION under FIRE

I have plans to hang out at a local club tonight and haven't had a chance to brief either of my partners of my unexpected—but filled with all kinds of possibilities—hookup. We were up well past midnight last night waiting for the conference call that did not happen.

Hopefully, JL can get us out of our current Airbnb contract today. If she can't, we had agreed she should go forward and line up another. We'll deal with the financial fallout later.

I left a note for JL, but it didn't mention my plans to meet up with my newly found friend, Sancheska—aka, SoS. In the meantime, I figure I'll make some more connections in the city. I'm sure that JaRew is doing the same.

SoS and I had no choice but to formally introduce ourselves to each other. How many times can you say "sorry" after invading the less than two inches of personal space between us? We didn't dare move too far to the left or right in order to maintain our front and center positions at the Big Daddy Kane concert. As it turned out, she was friends with DJ G8, who took us backstage to meet

Big Daddy himself. The DJ took shots of us with Big Daddy and gave us tickets to his next DJ event. I was excited to get a signed CD for my dad, and more importantly, that I now have some connections to the local community. JaRew and I had limited our concert communication to a few text messages. Hopefully, after tonight, I'll have some details worth sharing.

SoS and I plan to meet for lunch at Bombers, the café that had grabbed my attention on my ride through town when I first arrived. She insisted that the more than forty-five-minute wait would be well worth the café's "made to die for" burrito specialties. She chuckled when she gave me the heads-up. "Now, don't be late because we'll be pushing it to get to the mall in time for our mani-pedi appointments."

Anxious not to miss our scheduled appointment, I push the pedal to the metal, forcing the Escape to help me make up for lost time. The car speedometer tells me I'm at seventy-nine mph at the same time my rearview mirror warns me of the swirling blue lights a few miles back. Hoping against hope that the lights are not intended for me, I tap my brakes. The rental and I are now cruising at a comfortable sixty-five. The police car is less than a mile behind me, and the blue lights make it clear that I'm the culprit. My right signal light announces my intent to pull over, and I gradually move to the far-right lane and side of the road. The police car follows, mimicking my moves. I sigh and ignore the beep, "So whr r u?"

AFTER PUTTING my gearshift in park, I lower the window, accepting the inevitable. I freeze—nervous about making any unexpected moves and realize I've never been so skittish. When did I become such a scaredy-cat? And it's not like this is the first time I've been pulled over for speeding. According to my mother, I have a heavy foot just like my dad—and I can't disagree. But I'm a great driver and only exercise my race car driver mentality on straight highways with little traffic. Today is no exception. I'm loving the super well-paved straight stretch of Highway I-87. It's a beautiful road, and I hope I have the opportunity after the project to follow it all the way to the City of a Hundred Steeples—Mark Twain's nickname for Montreal. I've never been there, and I understand it's an incredible city. Per most respected travel logs, its 21stcentury skyline continues to showcase an endless supply of church and cathedral steeples. Steeples or not, Montreal, Canada is not on today's horizon.

I'm nervous. And there aren't many things in life that frighten me. Of course—past tense—that was my old life. Just yesterday, my new world forced me to not only confront but to accept my new reality. *I am not too young to die*. My STV reality show assures me that I'm not. I quickly reflect. I'm becoming unhinged. But why shouldn't I? I'm African American. I'm alone in suburban upstate New York and less than thirty miles from an unfamiliar community that's experiencing episodic spouts of violence. Episodic—defined as weekly. My hot, sweaty hands grip the even hotter steering wheel.

"Moving pretty fast there, Miss."

I keep my hands on the wheel and risk playing my usual game. "I believe I was just a few miles above the speed limit, wasn't I?"

"I need your license."

My hands are locked to the wheel. The officer hasn't cracked a smile.

"Can you please just ticket me?"

"I thought you weren't speeding." He's challenging me. I don't need this. Now, what do I do?

I quickly think *I'm not a Black male.* Maybe I'm okay. For the life of me, I can't remember the stats on African American women and police violence.

"Officer, can I take my hands down from the steering wheel?"

Stay cool, Blue Lady whispers.

Now I know I'm in trouble.

"Miss, I just need to see your license. Please."

I turn and look into his piercing deep brown eyes, searching for evidence of something.

Anger?

Venom?

Concern?

Authority?

Respect.

I hear my father's voice as clearly as if he's sitting next to me in the vehicle.

"Respect deserves respect, Ange. Always remember that."

"Is it safe for me to take my hands down, Officer? My wallet is in my purse."

"Miss, please. Your license?"

"Okay." I whisper a prayer, part of me knowing, or at least wanting to believe that I'm being paranoid. But what if I'm not?

I respond as I've been taught. As I would want someone to respond to me.

I'm not quite comfortable with the situation, but I decide to trust and get my license. After all, what other options do I really have? I slowly place my purse in my lap and look at the officer. "I'm going to get my wallet now, sir, and just so you know, I don't have a gun."

In the past, I would have expected him to smile at what I hoped he would have viewed as a weak joke. Why on earth would I be carrying a gun? Do I look like a gun-toter from the Gang of Roses?

I would have also flirted with him. He's a cutie. I can't help but notice that he wears his uniform well. He even walks with a slight swagger. I've flirted my way out of more tickets than I want to think about.

But today, I solemnly remove my license from my wallet and pass it to him through the open window. We both hear the beep. JaRew is getting impatient. He's probably worried since I haven't responded to the multiple messages.

I wonder what he would think if he knew I was sitting alongside the road waiting for a ticket.

The policeman takes my license, asks for my insurance card, and walks away.

"Sit tight. I'll be right back, Miss. And by the way, no need for you to sit there with your hands on the wheel."

Before I can respond, he walks off. Dang, I can't believe this—what a waste of time.

Beep! SoS again. "R u almost here?"

Afraid to pick up my phone, I shake my head at my carelessness. I don't have time for this—a fifteen-minute wait for a cop to call and check in with his Big Brother network.

I watch the officer approach through my rearview mirror. Well, that didn't take as long as I expected.

"Miss Mason?"

"Yes." I don't want to look at him for fear that my facial expression will get me in further trouble. "Can you just give me my ticket and let me go? Sir." I continue to stare ahead as though the balmy cumulus clouds before me asked the question. "Miss Mason, I clocked you at eighty-three miles an hour on a seventy mile-an-hour stretch. Much too fast, don't you think?"

I don't doubt him. I speak to the clouds, "Can you please just give me my ticket?"

"You're free to go, Miss Mason."

"Huh?"

"You're free to go."

"Huh? I mean—excuse me." I stutter my response. "You're-you're not giving me a ticket?"

I ignore the alternating text messages and wait for the officer to confirm his response. For the first time, I look at him. I mean, really look at him. This time, I see —and sense, the person and not the policeman.

"No, not today. Welcome to the great state of New York. But slow it down, Miss Mason. Be safe enough to visit us again, okay?"

"Oh, thank you. Thank you, Officer." I wanted to scream for joy. Instead, I say, "I truly appreciate it."

"You're welcome. But-."

"But?"

I can't believe it. He smiles—a contagious grin. I want to reciprocate, but for some reason, I conceal my natural reaction to his offer of what I don't know. If asked, I'm not sure I'd be able to explain why.

"But may I ask why, Officer?" I can't believe I'm questioning his decision.

"Why? Easy. I want you to enjoy your visit and come back to see us again, okay? Most importantly, please slow down. Be safe." He tips his hat and turns to walk away.

"Excuse me, Officer?"

As though sensing what I'm reluctant to articulate, he acknowledges, "Officer Pinkett."

This time I smile. "Officer Pinkett, thank you so much. You just made my day."

"Glad to do so, Miss Mason." He adds, "Remember… be safe."

CHAPTER ELEVEN

"It's getting' hot in here!"

"GOSH, I'M HOT!" I realize I'm yelling. I know I'm sweating. More importantly, I'm dancing like I've never danced before. I spin around in what I hope is in beat to the up-tempo, and I giggle when I think about how I must really look.

"Huh?" SoS leans over as she, too, shouts her response. With no exaggeration, the pounding beat of the drums reverberates from my feet to the top of my head. My hips swivel and shimmy to their own internal rhythm. I realize my body no longer belongs to me but is in sync with the jamming of a couple hundred people who are partying like there's no tomorrow.

"It's gettin' hot in here!" She nods and shrugs her shoulders. I don't bother to repeat the obvious.

Blue Lady's MISSION under FIRE

I raise my hands above my head, close my eyes, and move my head from side to side. I feel like a slithering cobra. No hissing, cause I'm loving every minute of it. I've made up my mind to live in the present. The moment. *This* moment. Who knows? This might be my last chance to dance. My last chance to slither.

"So, what do you think? Nice, huh?" SoS's elbow interrupts my flow as she whispers in my ear and spins away to the other side of me.

I slow to a competing rhythm. One that is now following my realization that this might just be the last time I dance. I want it to be slow and meaningful, I want to feel each beat. My reverie is interrupted by a loud clamoring call to action accompanied by a soft nudge on my waist.

"Clap! Clap! Clap, your hands!"

"Clap! Clap! Clap, your hands."

"Hey, I don't know how to do this." Somehow, I'm part of a huge line of dancers who all appear to know what they're doing, including SoS, who is three people over. The electric slide is the only line dance I know. And it's reserved for weddings and an occasional special birthday party I attend. This one's different— the steps are much more complicated.

I laugh at the guy next to me—the owner of the hands at my waist—guiding me to avoid collisions. I'm now face-to-face with him, which I realize isn't where I should be. He winks and gently turns me in the right position. Back in sync, SoS has somehow maneuvered herself so that she is in the line in front of me. I don't have time to figure out how she managed that move. As we rock back and forth in one of the few semi stationary parts of the dance, she leans over her right shoulder, "Hey, spin left." My mystery partner taps my waist from behind. After a few more rounds and with his gentle guidance, I smile and yell, "All right, I got it!"

"Get it, gurl." SoS grins as she pulls back her long hair that is now as straight as mine is frizzy. I bet she'll twist hers up and on top with the shortest pause in the music. Mine will do its thing regardless of my plucking and pulling, so I don't bother. This time I turn, expecting to be greeted by my newfound friend, but instead, find myself head to chest with

Jude Hinkley. What the heck is he doing here? Not again. This is definitely not a coincidence. Wait until JaRew hears about this.

He puckers his lips as though he intends to deliver an unexpected, but more importantly, unwanted kiss. I spin around. Our bodies almost touch on the wiggle room-only dance floor. I hear SoS, who manages to squeeze behind me. "Who is *that*?"

I shrug my shoulders, surprised at her hint of interest but dismiss the thought immediately.

"Oops." My dance teacher has returned. I almost collide with him and the two drinks he's carrying. He hands me a shot glass. The DJ shouts over the music, "It's tequila-shot time." I've never drank tequila and never taken a "shot" of anything—not even the Jell-O shot at my friend, Dee Dee's bachelorette party. The choice is simple. Take the shot or figure out another way to avoid Jude. I don't know what he's thinking, but he knows the rules as well as I do. Team members are not to be seen in public with each other. I wonder what game he's playing. He's now dancing with SoS, and they've just toasted each other before downing their shots. It looks like Mr. Hinkley is ready to party. From the looks of his bloodshot eyes and disheveled appearance, he's already partied. Not certain what to do, I turn away, now face-to-face with my partner, who lifts his glass in a toast to me. "To us," he mouths. I groan and wonder just what I've gotten myself into. My partner takes my shot glass and dances away, giving me time to think.

So, what's Hinckley really up to? Jude is the odd man out. But he must be bringing something to the table. He's older than the rest of the team. He speaks like a college professor and normally walks like a celebrity on the red carpet. *So much for first impressions.*

Tonight, he's more than casual. He's sloppy. His shirt is hanging outside of his khaki slacks. He wears a tie, but it's untied. His wavy silver-streaked hair looks as though it hasn't seen a comb or brush in days.

As though reading my mind, Jude abruptly spins and weaves his way to the other side of the dance floor. His six-foot-plus height and the neon-colored laser lights glittering on his silver-streaked hair make it even easier for me to track his moves. From what I can see, he passes the bar and appears to be heading for the exit. SoS, however, is nowhere in sight. The music slows as Keith Sweat begs, "Make it last forever."

"Care to dance, Lady?"

I shrug my shoulders in response to my dance partner, who comes and goes on a second's notice. Looking for an excuse to say, 'Thanks, but no thanks,' I say, "And what do you propose I do with this?" He'd handed me another shot.

"I'd say chug it—like this!" He smiles, dazzling me with his exotic, mesmerizing stare. Before I can answer, he downs his drink, wipes his mouth with the back of his hand, and taunts, "I dare you."

I return his stare, entranced not only by his voice but also his dare. I think about it for a second, chug the drink and hand him my glass. He sets the shot glasses on the nearest table and wraps his muscular, chocolate brown arms around me. I lay my head against his chest —his chin massages the top of my head. Wow, it's *really* getting hot in here.

I sigh. What the heck am I doing? I don't know, but it feels good. Warm but pleasant is how my body responds to my dance partner's embrace. I don't know his name, but I like his company. I've never had a fling, but for some reason, this guy makes me think I could. I fall into this stranger's arms as though I've known him for years. Keith keeps us company in our world.

I'm startled when I hear SoS's giggle. Who's she talking to? Jude Hinkley's sophisticated baritone answers my question. I don't dare turn to look. I don't want to see.

CHAPTER TWELVE

"I've got to go!"

THOUGH SULTRY, the night air refreshes me. Warm but not stifling. I fan myself with my hand as though that will help. I have no idea where we're heading. Those shots must have been pretty potent. I pull away from my Childish Gambino lookalike. He grabs my hand, obviously expecting a part two to this evening. I check my Fitbit. Two a.m. OMG. My message pop-ups go bonkers on me. JaRew. JI. Cooke. My dad. Cooke.

JaRew. *I've got to go.*

"I've got to go."

I stop, snatch my hand from my charming dance partner's and wait for SoS and Jude to catch up with us. It didn't take them long since they were only a few feet behind.

I ignore Jude. He ignores me.

"Hey, you ready, S? I didn't know it was so late. I've got to go."

"I'm ready. Sorry, Hink, I've got to go. Nice to meet you."

"It was nice to meet you, as well."

My dance partner leans over and whispers, "Can I get your number? A name would be nice, too." He winks. I notice for the first time the huge—at least twenty-five carat—diamond hanging from the equally impressive platinum chain. Marilyn would be proud of her daughter.

I smile with no intent to give up the digits—my version of street lingo—and I don't have a name to give, so why does my alter ego offer up her two cents?

"Blue."

"Nice to meet you, Blue. Anything to do with those sapphire earrings?" His smile is as sweet as my grandmother's blueberry cobbler.

Omission number three: no attention-wearing clothing. We'd discussed this, but I opted to wear my studs, making the argument to myself that I have to look like a girl dressed up for clubbing. Skinny jeans. Slinky stilettos. The studs I'm never without. Blue Lady lets me have it at this point. *Did you even consider a nice pair of silver hoops? You have a long way to go, kiddo.*

Within minutes, SoS and I had ditched our dance partners, thanked them for a great evening, and dodged the question of whether there would be a next time.

"YEAH, I'M GOOD." S and I wobble across the parking lot. I kick myself for my decision to forgo valet parking. S had volunteered to pay the fifteen dollars since I had driven, but I said it would be a waste of her hard-earned money and suggested she buy the first round of drinks.

The warm but now breezy fall night cools my body, and I realize I really don't miss Hot-Lanta's humidity, but I do miss the cicadas. Sorta, kinda— since a sledgehammer has taken up residence in my head. I press my fingers against my forehead in an effort to lessen the pounding.

S and I steady ourselves. We support each other as we remove our stilettos, both realizing we'll never make it to the Escape at the back of the now semi deserted parking lot without toppling over. Due to the size of the crowd, I had parked on a grassy hill, so barefootin' was the only way to go—making it much easier to navigate.

"I can't tell you the last time I had so much fun." I giggle, evidence of too many tequila shots.

"Me, either." SoS laughs. "I'm not really a party animal, but I love to dance, and music is my thing." I feel the shove before I hear the shots.

CHAPTER THIRTEEN

"It sounds like a synchronized duet to me."

"HEY, BLUE LADY, can you tell me what made you decide that sapphire blue earrings are appropriate accessories for an undercover girl from down the way?" JL shakes her head.

I remove my studs and place them on the napkin next to my coffee cup. My head pounds. The three thirty a.m. dosage of Tylenol has done nothing to apologize to my system for the overindulgence. JL made breakfast, the looks of which make my stomach churn.

JaRew follows his usual morning routine and skims the local, NYS, and national headlines. In that order. Google has again done its homework. One word: "Shootings" populates a list of more shooting incidents than I want to know about—even on a good day of research. I'm not at all surprised when JaRew reads aloud, "Shooting at Local Casino."

"Oh, no!" I groan and without thinking, add, "Can you read me the details? Oops."

JaRew peers across the table at me. I'm unsuccessful at avoiding his hazel-eyed accusation.

"Hey, Blue, please don't tell me you were there."

I hold my head, rubbing it gently, promising if it behaves, I'll never drink a shot of tequila again.

Nothing like a vengeful Blue Lady. *Liar!*

"And don't call me Blue! Please." I continue massaging my temples.

"And why are you rubbing your head? What's wrong? Are you all right?"

JL's frown and Blue Lady's internal prompting warn me to back off.

"And since when can't I call you Blue?"

I decide to confess. If I don't, my alter ego will. I've learned the hard way that it's better for me to speak for myself. My doppelganger says some things I'd never say. And definitely, in a way I'd never say them. I'm no longer surprised when she pipes up: *Like drink tequila shots, perhaps? Fess up time, right?* I stop short of calling her a traitor because she's saved me from myself more times than I can count. As usual, this morning, she shows up when I least expect. But I don't need her now. I decide to break the news gently. Myself.

JL joins us at the table after refilling our coffee cups. Her expression, too, clearly reveals her spoken aloud thoughts. "I can't wait to hear this."

"Me either," JaRew adds while continuing his search. I sip my coffee, deciding to play this out for as long as I can. I need time to think. How much of last night should I tell?

"JL, let me bring you up to speed. She never showed up at the racetrack last night. Did you forget our plans, Blue?" He shakes his head. "And you're not going to believe who I ran into. I got lucky, too."

"All I want to know is how much did you win?" JL asks. And before he can answer, she adds, "Don't tell me Jude was at the track."

"None-a-ya! And yep!" He pulls out a wad of bills from his pants pocket, unfolds them and waves them at us for our viewing pleasure. "I'm not really a gambler, but yesterday, I decided to try my luck.

And I don't know if Jude saw me or not. He sat trackside with a pair of binoculars hanging around his neck. I won't attempt to describe the snazzy multi-colored neck strap." JaRew laughed and added, "Yeah, he appeared to be by himself, too. He looked pleasant enough. He guzzled a few suds, and, by the way, no tie yesterday."

I groan when I realize I'd totally forgotten about our hastily made plans to scout out the Saratoga Race Track.

"Glad you had a good time." I know I've goofed when JL not only ignores my comment but doesn't bother to look my way as she resettles herself at the table.

"Sorry about the change of plans JaRew, but…" I clear the imaginary gook in my throat. "I had some good luck myself yesterday. You guys aren't going to believe this, but I met this really cool girl at the Big

Daddy Kane concert the other night and —"

"I saw her." JaRew pecks away as his search intensifies.

"Who is she?

103

"What does she do?

"Where does she live? "What did you tell her?"
I count to ten.

"Where do you want me to start? Hold on a sec.
I'll be right back."

I stand and trot to the kitchen for a bottle of
water —definitely time to hydrate. *No more shots,* I
chide myself.

When I return, I see four accusatory eyes
tracking my every move. JL shakes her head again.
I wish she'd stop. She's not making this any easier. I
know I flubbed up.

I fill them in.

The plan to meet up for lunch and the nail shop.

Shopping at the mall.

The dancing.

The good time.

Seeing Jude.

Not a word about the shots.

The dancing.

The even better good time.

Seeing Jude.

The off-the-cuff creation of my street name.

The walk to the rental.

Our long-term commitment to full disclosure overpowers me.

The shots.

"You have got to be kidding me." I truly can't tell if they both say the same words at the same time, but it sounds like a synchronized duet to me.

"Unfortunately, I'm not. But—"

JL again shakes her head and adds, "It could have been worse."

I nod my head—time to hydrate. I finish off my bottle of water.

BOTH THE *ALBANY TIMES UNION* and *Schenectady Gazette* cover the story. Apparently, two men were hospitalized from gunshot wounds in the valet parking area. It sounds like my decision to park on the grass was a wise one.

I confess that an undefined "we" were leaving the casino when we heard the shots. I don't reveal that "my" mystery man had not only followed us surreptitiously to the parking lot but shoved me to the ground, wrapping his arms around me to protect me from an onslaught of bullets. I can still hear the reverberation of shots as I share my version of the local news.

Although I have mixed feelings about sharing the little tête-à-tête between SoS and Jude, I decide it might be best to confide since I can't explain how Jude appeared out of nowhere and just happened to buddy up with "S." I had to think it through, but I also know I have to share it with my partners. I accept that I'm out of my league on this stuff. And while I'm accustomed to doing things my way, I know the importance of making my way *our* way. I no longer trust Beckham. And I don't want JaRew and JL to view me as another Beckham. Furthermore, I know we will fail in our team effort if we don't work together on something so complex and important. I realize it's no longer about me, Cooke, or even Beckham—it's much bigger than that. It's about *our* opportunity to make things better.

Blue Lady gently reminds me that I can't conquer the world. And she's right, but I can do my best to make it a better place. I trust my two 'Js'. And

I don't want to do anything to cause them to think they can't trust me. It's fess-up time.

CHAPTER FOURTEEN

"What makes you think I'm the target?"

JAREW GROANS AND grimaces at me from across the room at the sound of Lionel Richie's melodious, "Hello." I ignore him and my dad's call deciding this was not the best time to chat with either. A part of me wants to share the details of the project with my father—in particular, Beckham's double-dealing—but decide that this is not the time to do so. Neither of my housemates asks the obvious, but I share, "My dad. I'll call him later."

I'm not surprised by their silence. Rather than follow up, I direct my attention to the majestic gold framed seascape that offered serenity and tranquility, unlike the tension that permeates the room. Nice, I think.

Both he and JL are angry that I dared to venture out into unknown territory with someone I'd just met. Shaking his head, JaRew continues his internet search.

Based on his disparaging expression, though, it's hard for me to read him.

Does he honestly believe that some community thug was out to get me last night? Or does he think I should have taken Dad's call?

Or is he responding in his usual fashion to my ringtone? He's shared his distaste of Richie, one of my favorite entertainers, on more occasions than I care to think about. No reason to think today is an exception. It's only one of the many facets of our differing personality quirks—the kind that is common to a solid friendship such as ours.

JaRew's dislike of the singer has nothing to do with his voice, musical repertoire—not even his appearance or style of dress. Per JaRew, Lionel Richie is an Alabamian. End of subject!

He's never answered my why as to his deep, dark feelings about the state of Alabama. I've decided he'll share with me when he's ready. If he were in a better mood, I'd respond with a "Roll Tide," but I don't want to take him over the edge. Normally, I could expect a chuckle. But he's so immersed in his research on the shooting and trying to figure out if I could have been a target last night, I realize it's no time to play games.

I can't follow his logic on this one. Who'd be tracking me? Other than Desmond Cooke or Beckham, who'd be looking for me? I was just one of many diners at the Cheesecake Factory the other afternoon. And what's so special about me that I would stand out from anyone else in the over-the-top crowd at the Five Alive Concert? It would take much more than my sapphire earrings to get someone's attention. *So you think.*

"Question folks, what *are* we really doing here? Do I get a chance to meet Beckham? What about this Dez Cooke you're both so fond of?" When neither the walls nor seascape respond, JL excuses herself to take a shower. I take advantage of her absence to settle my thoughts. JaRew continues his ongoing love affair with his laptop.

JL's inquiry causes me to reexamine my behavior since JaRew, and I unceremoniously dumped Cooke's "trap" phones. I'd ignored the one call I'd received from Beckham, but my Sunday School upbringing unsettled my spirit. I owe him so much. Forgiveness Lane is just a few days down the road. I already know what I have to do.

"I guess I'm talking to myself, huh?" JL continues her train of thought as though she'd never left the room.

"You're right, JL. I just haven't figured out what to say. JaRew—?"

"I suggest you don't ask me." He doesn't even bother to look up as though the laptop is speaking to him.

"Anybody want more coffee? Fresh brew, yours for the asking. I just made a pot."

"I would." JaRew jots down a few notes in his handy notebook and continues his search. A sure sign he's onto something.

"Me, too. But I can get it, JL."

"Don't worry about it. I've got it, Ange. I gotchu, too, Jarewski." She heads down the narrow hallway of our new Airbnb. Unlike me, JL had taken care of her assignment. From my semi long-distance peek at JaRew's list of phone numbers, his diligence must be paying off. Wow! How can my team be ahead of its leader?

JL carefully sets the teal blue tray in the center of the farmhouse style dining room table, not wanting to tip over the full carafe of coffee. Consistent with the Suzy Homemaker side of her personality, she'd added a few Dunkin' Donuts, a saucer of fresh fruit, and napkins.

Standing with her hands on her hips, she adds. "Nobody's asked me, but I strongly recommend you guys touch base with somebody. And soon." She turns to head back to the kitchen but reverses her steps. Guess she's decided she needs a face to face with us. She obviously believes we didn't get her point when she emphatically points out, "I don't really know what the two of you are doing, but I do know you need to touch base with the project team. You may not *want* to talk with Cooke, but you *need* to talk with him. And soon. Unless you want him showing up on your doorstep. Or should

I say *our* doorstep? By the way, do either of them know I'm now part of your package deal?"

JaRew looks at me. I sigh, embarrassed that I've been so busy having a good time that I've neglected my team. *And you accuse Beckham of disloyalty?* When Blue Lady opts to join the discussion, I know I'm in trouble. They're right.

"You don't have to answer, Ange. I already know the deal—but I don't think you're getting this—any of this stuff. And I'm so, so serious—as a heart attack, as they say. Forgive me, Hun. And not to be insensitive, but I know that you know the significance of a heart that threatens to stop beating."

JaRew pivoted—a sharp ninety-degree bona fide head and shoulder jerk—shocked at JL's inference to my dad's recent heart attack and obviously concerned about how I might react.

"Based on what you told me, I wouldn't be shocked if Cooke surprises us with a visit. And he won't necessarily wait for one of us to open that beautiful and obviously recently installed front door, either." She flounces back to the kitchen and from the slamming of the cabinet doors—also obviously newly installed—I know she is more than miffed. JaRew, who speaks Spanish, looks over at me. "And you don't want to know what she's saying."

JL returns from her unofficial time out. This time, she wheels in a serving cart and sits. Her message is, obviously, *serve yourselves*. JaRew does and chomps into an apple as he reviews his handwritten notes.

"In case either of you wants to know, I met with a staffer from the governor's office yesterday. She gave me the scoop on the new NYS grants. The state has received funds from the feds, and it looks like Albany may be seeking funds to support a local Give Peace a Chance project."

I guess she has second thoughts and decides to refresh our coffee cups. "If anyone cares, I recommend a meeting with Cooke's uncle. His name was mentioned in the meeting." Why do they both look at me?

Now, I'm really embarrassed. Both of my team members are out front and ahead of me. Blue Lady is right. I've let my hurt feelings and emotions drive my actions—actions that are no longer focused on our goal.

I know my face is flushed because my body is warm. "Wow. I don't know what to say, JL. I'm-I'm so sorry—"

"Thank you is more than enough."

"I'm not referring to the coffee, JL. But thank you. I appreciate it and your support," I mumble softly before adding what I know I need to say.

"But I'm sorry, JL. You, too, JaRew. I don't know what's come over me." *Yes, you do. You're afraid you're going to die*—Blue Lady's right.

"Thanks for the coffee, JL. She's on point, Boss Lady. You need to call Cooke. Forget Beckham for now. I hope you know Cooke's already given him the 411. Beckham knows you chucked those phones. And didn't you say, you haven't returned his calls? You're right; the chump owes you an explanation. But how can he give it if you don't call him?" He hesitates and adds, "Just remember, though, when and if you decide to follow up, that jerk owes *you* the explanation and not vice versa." His poignant stare says what he doesn't.

I sigh but don't respond to Jarewski's backhanded punch. He knows I'm hurt by Beckham's transgression. He makes it clear he's done with the conversation for now when he stands and stretches. His white Hanes T-shirt rises, revealing a six-pack I would have never known he had. He's obviously quite comfortable with his casual attire. I check the vee on my graphic tee shirt to ensure I'm not broadcasting an unintended message, avert my eyes, and hear his loud yawn. JL winks when she notices my gesture.

JaRew reclaims the desk chair in the corner alcove — the one and only official workstation in the house.

He'd staked his territory immediately upon our arrival.

"I'll print you out a copy of the grant guidelines, JL. I was down at city hall yesterday myself. My contact seems to think we might have a shot at the funding, too."

"I agree with JaRew, Ange. And like I said, we need to meet with Cooke's uncle."

I was blown away. Isn't there an award-winning grant writer in the room? Blue Lady is fed up with me too: *Last time I checked, there was. And guess what, unless she picks up her pace, she won't have a shot at this funding opportunity.*

CHAPTER FIFTEEN

"You saw that the cops haven't found the shooter, right?"

"JUST A FEW MORE MINUTES, Blue. My part-timer should be here to cover for me soon. Hey, actually, I'm surprised to see you. Let me get you a cup of coffee."

"Surprised? Why is that? Didn't we—"

Oops, she just called me Blue. *You've got more important things to worry about. And did you forget the two of you were caught in crossfire last night? Unless JaRew is right—this just might be a good time to get a second opinion. Were you the bullseye for those FMJs that whizzed over your head? Or was your new bestie the intended prize trophy? Or was someone aiming their Saturday night special at a two-fer-one deal? Was it a lone wolf? Or a gang of wolves? Duh. You show up for an afternoon of shopping as though you had the time of your life last night. Did you forget both of you could have been killed? Except for sheer luck, it could have been the last friggin' good time of your life.*

OMG! It's time for me to step to the plate, be present, and accounted for. Darn. *How many times have you said that recently, Angelica?*

SoS winks and continues, "Yeah, after last night. I'm so sorry. We were having such a good time, too. Our cool guy hookups were something else, weren't they? And handsome—creamy vanilla and chocolate swirl eye candy."

I nod not quite certain of what I should—or shouldn't say. But I didn't need to worry. Unlike me, SoS is on a roll.

"And I so wanted you to enjoy your first official night out on the town, Blue. Just unbelievable. But that's the nature of our world these days. At least my world." She sighs as though to reflect upon her out of personal control universe and continues, "So, how do you feel? My right leg is sore. I scraped my knee when I hit the ground. Hey, did you see this morning's paper?" She passes me one of several

119

well-read copies of the *Times Union* along with a cup of coffee.

I slide onto the stool, mumble "Thanks," and struggle to regroup, using the time it takes to skim the article to gather my thoughts.

Am I dumb or what?

Dumb is right. I couldn't have said it better.

"Hey, S. Shocked that you remember my nickname." I ignore Blue Lady's sarcasm and offer up a girly giggle since I can't figure out how to navigate the ship that seems to have sprung a slow leak. "Despite it all, we had a good time last night, right?"

"Um, yeah, I guess so. My head is killing me. I just took two Tylenol." She frowns as she refills what appears to be the last of the condiment containers on her purple laminated counter. "So, you plan to stick around? You saw that the cops haven't found the shooter, right?"

Uh-oh. Not good. How do I respond? *Sure, won't be leaving until I figure out what I'm supposed to be doing. And then, depending on the game plan, I might still be in town.*

On the other hand, maybe I won't.

"Ummm, not finished reading yet. But no scrubbed knees for me. Oh, so the police determined that it was just one shooter?" I stall for time by feigning a reread of the article that the team and I had dissected for information and insight all morning.

Before I can mull over her question and my tepid response and figure out what might be an appropriate follow-up, she adds, "I'm surprised that you showed up today—you're tougher than you look, I guess. You fooled me."

Duh—I'm blowing it. Again. Instead of picking up the biggest bat and stepping to the plate like an A-Rod, is she suggesting I should have made my reentry today like the cowardly lion? Blue Lady pipes up, *Maybe. Especially since you're afraid to die— and so is she, or have you forgotten Westchester County?*

Ugh...I refuse to let my alter ego take me there. Not now. Hoping I sound tougher than I feel, I respond, "Oh, really?"

She shrugs her shoulders. "Food is what you need. It always makes me feel better. I have a fresh fruit platter —the healthy option. Or, if you'd like something to stick to your bones, I have some fried chicken." She winks.

I'm impressed with SoS's pop-up. It's not far from the neighborhood laundromat, where I met my friend Jaylen and his mom. I make no further pretense of reading the paper, and she obviously feels no need to continue our chitchat. Normally, I'd take the fresh fruit platter as I'm sure she expects. "I'll take an order of the fried chicken to go. May I have an order of cheese fries, too, please? Oh, and don't forget the hot sauce." My turn to wink.

The cheerful, young customer who enters smiles at me. "A lady who knows what's good. Nothing like some fried chicken. SoS's wing special is the best. Yummy!"

"Hey, Nisha. Perfect timing. Hey Blue, meet Janisha —one of my regulars. Your order's ready, Nish. See you tomorrow!"

"Will do, SoS. You know I depend on you. Heading to the gym. Hey, don't forget—you're on for your presentation next weekend, right? Dr.

Washington finally signed off on the program. I know it's taken forever, but I hope you're still free."

The proud University of Albany student grins and flips her long, blue, middle-of-the-back tresses over her shoulder, balancing her snack pack in her other hand. I chuckle as I notice that her hair matches the deep blue and gold university colors.

"I'm good. Wouldn't miss it. I'll text you a list of 'must-haves' for the girls, okay? Oh, and yeah, I need to know exactly where we're meeting."

"Great! Wow, I didn't think we'd ever get the signoff. With all the drama around here, you'd think they'd want everybody to take your course."

"Hmmm, would be nice, Nisha. But you have to start somewhere."

"I know..."

"Now is not the time to give up, Nisha. You've got your foot through the door."

SoS waves goodbye, then checks her watch and the front door as though her part-timer may have magically appeared. Frowning, this time, she confers with the eye-catching purple and silver wall clock as though questioning the accuracy of her watch. Hmmm, my new friend has style. Purple. I like it. She returns to her busy work and her efforts to minimize the amount of clean-up she leaves for her part-timer. I take advantage of one of the twin lawn chairs out front, noticing for the first time the matching lavender and white set. I pull my sunglasses from my bag and sip from the extra-large perfectly blended homemade lemonade. I'm tempted to savor one of the spicy, sweet-smelling chicken wings but refrain. Messy, messy, messy. How can I people watch with barbecue sauce dribbling down my chin?

CHAPTER SIXTEEN

"Should we pray about it?"

MY BOUGIE BACKGROUND isn't as conspicuous as it was upon my arrival—at least, I don't think it is. JL had given me some makeup tips but had been so disgusted with my proudly handpicked new makeup choices that she coerced me to sit with her as she perused the MAC online site. I admit she didn't need to twist my arm when we landed on MAC's frost lipstick line—Designer Blue, a deep ocean blue shade was made for me. Now I fully understand JL's scowl when she saw the burgundy tracks the hairstylist had weaved into my naturally black hair. "Blue" needs to sport deep blue tracks...like Nisha's. I imitate Nisha's fly girl neck/shoulder wiggle. Another nightmare for Mother Marilyn. Thank God, she'll never see my urban dancer video image—pointed, long metallic blue nails included. I laugh again when I can't resist the urge to reexamine my look. I rummage through my new Urban Legend hobo bag for my makeup mirror and purse my lips at the thought of refreshing my makeup sitting out on the block, as it is frequently called. Oh, yeah! There's hope for the homegirl, after all.

SOS HAD BOUGHT into my partially true story that I'd lost my job, wanted a change of scenery, and was looking for employment in the NYS Legislature. My heavy southern twang validated my Southern girl roots. S brings me a fresh lemonade, giggling. "This will hold you over until later."

"Thanks. By the way, what's the program you're running for the Albany State girls?" I slurp my drink.

"Self-defense. I have a black belt."

"Wow!" Hmmm, now that's interesting. I would have never guessed. Maybe I do need to keep my eyes open. JaRew could be right. "That's cool. Maybe I can visit the class?"

"Sure, I don't see why not. I'd love for you to join us. I'll check first with Nisha to make sure we don't violate any of the college's protocols, okay?"

"Sounds like a plan." I dismiss any doubts I had about S. To teach the class, I'm sure she had to provide her credentials and submit to a background check. I don't wait for Blue Lady to interject on this one. I'm comfortable with my decisive conclusion. S is a down the way girl, but she's all right with me.

"This lemonade is so good. You've got something a little different in it. Can't name it."

She winks. "My special brew. SOS Special." She giggles and adds. "Nutcrackers, for my special friends."

Oh well, maybe there's another side to my new friend. I text JaRew, deciding it doesn't hurt to check. "What's a nutcracker?"

"Hey, Lady Sancheska."

I look up from my phone and almost choke.

"Hey, Mr. Pope. How are you today?"

Marcus Pope. How the heck does he know S? I don't know what to say, so I say nothing. I focus my attention on the dripping lemon slice in my hand and not the sparkling diamond in Pope's ear.

"Do you need a tissue, Miss?"

I sputter a thank you and accept the tissue. S gives me a "what's up" look and passes me a few more.

I accept the second couple of vivid purple, SOS engraved napkins with a mumbled, "Thank you."

I don't want to know what S is thinking at this point. No time to focus on her thoughts when mine are running as wild as a renegade bull in a rodeo competition.

"Mr. Pope, this is my friend, Blue. Blue, meet Mr. Pope. He's new in town, too."

"Hello, Blue, and Sancheska, will you please stop calling me Mr. Pope? I know I'm older than you, but not that old."

I join in their laughter and decide to play the game.

"Nice to meet you, umm, Mr. Pope, is it?"

I smile at my rejoinder, not knowing what to expect from Pope.

"Not you, too. C'mon, ladies. Can't you give the stranger in town a break?"

All right, it looks like we're good.

"So, what brings you to Albany, Marcus? I'll be kind. I know how it feels to be the new kid on the block."

"Now, that's more like it." He smiles.

S pipes up. "He's here working with some of our community groups. It's a shame that people like Mr. … Umm, oh sorry…people like Marcus have to come into town to help us resolve our community problems." She shook her head and continued. "How did your meeting go with the mayor? Was the police chief there?"

Wow! It looks like somebody's been on the move. I'm wondering when's the last time he checked in with Cooke? I text JaRew. "We need to talk. ASAP!"

I don't have to wait long. "Yep. Guess who I just ran into?"

Well, I know who he isn't with but decide not to respond, tuning in to Pope's exchange with S.

"That's what I do, Sancheska, and Albany is not the only town facing these kinds of problems. I just left Chicago, where there was another big shooting."

"Where are you from, Marcus? And just what is it that you do?" I dare to ask, thinking we're supposed to be on the same team. Isn't this the way it's played?

"I guess you could say I'm a community organizer. It's in my blood. My grandfather actually marched in Selma with Dr. King."

I wonder if he just made that up. "I bet you have a lot of stories to tell."

He eyeballs me. "I do." Marcus opens a leather cross shoulder bag that swung low on his hips.

"Nice chatting with you, ladies. Sancheska, I just stopped by to ask if I can leave these flyers with you. We're holding a community vigil and prayer meeting next week. We're doing everything we can to get people interested, out, and to the table. Can I count on you to help spread the word?"

"Sure. What else can I do?"

He grins and removes the dark glasses that I'd never seen him without. "I was hoping you'd ask. I have an idea." He smiles and looks at me. "Have you tried the SoS Special Wing Combo, Blue?"

Not yet, but I have tried the SOS Special Nutcracker. It must have been pretty potent because, for the first time, I realize just how handsome Marcus is. It's got to be the lemonade cause he's not my type. And I never mix business with pleasure. I feel this kick —aka, Blue Lady's at it. *You need to calm down. Shawn, Beckham. And what's going on with you and JaRew? And now, Pope? What does that make you, Ms. Blue? One Blue talkin' to another. Just sayin'.*

"No, not yet, but what do her wings have to do with the prayer vigil?" I snap and check myself. Based on both of their facial expressions, I realize my reaction may have been inappropriate. I don't know what's wrong with me. I quite plainly hear: *I do.*

"You may have been away from the hood a little too long." His initial smile becomes a grin. He's making fun of me.

Blue Lady's MISSION under FIRE

"Actually, maybe you've never been in the hood, but guess what? You have been hungry. You know what good food tastes like. I'm sure your parents and friends have hosted some highfalutin—as my parents might say—events. The menu may not have included spicy chicken wings, fried fish, and potato salad, but we don't need caviar to comfort the souls of hurting people." S covers her mouth, not quite sure what to say.

I'm speechless. I guess I'm not the only one with a dual personality. This is my first time seeing this, Mr. Pope. Another part of me wants to believe he's faking a move. The pang in the center of my chest, however, convinces me that he's sincere. If he's not, then he's in the wrong field. He should head out to Hollywood. To make matters worse, he decides to give me a lesson on the problems the community is facing.

"Maybe you ladies don't know the scope and magnitude of the problems this city is facing. You may not have heard yet, and this is confidential, but Reverend Shabazz and I were up at St. Peter's Hospital last night with the parents of a young man

132

who was shot and fatally wounded two weeks ago. Their seventeen-year-old daughter decided to end it all rather than wait around to become the city's next victim. She's hanging on by a thread. Please keep her in your prayers."

I know he pauses for impact because he stares me down for what seems like ten minutes without saying another word. S busies herself by reading and rereading, shuffling and reshuffling the stack of flyers.

"So, what's a few hot wings gonna do? You're right, in the overall scheme of things, not much. But they might just make somebody think that somebody cares." He turns as though to walk away.

S asks, "How many wings?"

"As many as you can contribute. I hope we have a few hundred people. Turnout has not been good at the last couple of meetings, though. People are petrified. And I can understand why. I'm looking for some businesses to contribute to our 'Should We Pray About It?' tee shirt project."

"I can handle that, Marcus."

He looks at me as though I have two heads. "Handle what?"

"The tee shirts."

He's obviously unprepared for my response, but that's his problem. Figure it out, teammate. Two can play this game.

"How many do you need?"

He hesitates. "A few hundred, I guess."

"Have they been designed?"

"No, I—"

"I've got it covered. A thousand—specially designed. Just let me know what you want them to say. Can't get them done in time for the vigil, but I'll have them for you in three weeks. Will that work?"

"I don't know what to say."

"You don't have to say anything. If you have more of those flyers, I'll be happy to distribute some of them. I'll bring some snack packs for the kids, too."

I don't know who is playing who in this tripartite scenario. But maybe we have more in common than we think. Our actions will support the vigil. And that's what counts. For now.

CHAPTER SEVENTEEN

"Who said it would be easy?"

WE WATCH as Marcus walks down the street, passing out flyers, stopping to periodically chat with an interested bystander.

S shakes her head and hesitates before speaking, obviously unsure of what to say or not say. I speak, not knowing what else to do at this point.

"Nice guy, huh?"

"Yeah, he seems to be. Hey, the two of you might be a good match."

"Excuse me?"

S smiles at me and shrugs her shoulders. "You never know. You guys seem to have some kind of vibe going on. And yes, he seems like a nice guy. I don't really know him...he's only been in town for a short time. But people like him, and they can relate to him." Her violet eyes search mine as though looking for answers that I already know I won't be able to provide.

"So, what makes you think we'd be a good match?" What did I reveal? Maybe I'm too upfront to take on this undercover stuff.

"I don't know..." She clears her throat as though opening a constricted path from her soul to her lips. "You just seem to click. That discussion about the tee shirts and the upcoming event—even the chicken wings."

She laughs like she's having a good ole time, as my dad would say...and at my expense. Nothing's funny at all to me at this point. Beckham will never forgive me if I botch the project. I've been known to blush and hope my cheeks and forehead aren't giving me away. "You felt something. Didn't you?" She doesn't wait for me to respond. "You had to. I know you did." She nudges me. "You had to feel something. Why else would you volunteer to donate all those friggin' tee shirts?"

"Yeah, I know. What was I thinking?" I roll my eyes and shrug my shoulders, hoping she buys my play dumb maneuver. But she's right. I did feel something. Marcus was so convincing. But convincing does not make one trustworthy. I make a mental note to touch base with JaRew to see what he might know about this guy's background.

"ON ANOTHER NOTE, there's something I need to tell you."

I had just been ready to remind S of our appointments, but the urgency in her voice cautions me to wait and listen. "What's up?"

"Well, it's gotten to the point where I don't always feel safe around here. I hate to say it, and I don't want to discourage you—you know, with you being new to Albany and all. But it's just not the same as it was when I first moved here from the city."

"Oh, really? What's changed?" I know, but I want her to tell me anyway.

She looks around as though searching for something or someone and waits for an attractive arm in arm couple to stroll pass before continuing.

Her lowered voice warns that she plans to share what she believes to be a big, dark secret. "It's as though Albany is under attack."

"Huh? Attack?" I hope my voice disguises the fear I thought I had deep-sixed. What kind of attack is she talking about?

"Yeah," she whispers and continues, "The shootings. You know, right?"

I nod my head, careful to conceal how much I really know. My body tenses when I think there could have been even another shooting.

"A lot of people have died. It's strange. And I left New York City to get away from violence. Weird."

"Weird? What's weird about you leaving to get away from—"

"'Cause I feel like it followed me, almost as though I'm in the middle of it."

"Ohhhh." I freeze, not knowing what to say and hope my tone conceals the personal anxiety I feel. I encourage her to continue. "I'm so sorry." It works.

"I left New York City after my cousin was shot and killed right in front of my uncle's garage on Westchester Avenue in the Bronx. I'll never forget it.

One Saturday afternoon—a typical Saturday in the city— music, shoppers, kids slurping their Kool Pops."

I risk interrupting the flow of her thoughts with another expression of my concern. A very heartfelt one. "I'm so sorry, S."

"Thanks. Yeah, it got crazy after that. Yep, I decided to get the heck out. The escalating violence was too much for me to handle even though I love the city's vibe. I'm definitely a NYC girl, as the song says, but I had no choice. There's still so much I want to do." She sighs and continues as we walk to our cars.

"When I finished school, my mother reached out to her best friend who lives over in Troy, right across the river. I lived with her for about a year while I got on my feet, found a job, and saved some money."

I learn that her brother also lives in the area. Apparently, he's doing well for himself. He owns several businesses, and from her description, he seems to be a mover and a doer. According to S, his vision is to "buy up the block"—his words. I don't press her for details, but she makes it clear that she and her brother have different business goals. I don't ask how or why they differ, holding my questions for another time and place.

To my surprise, she murmurs, "And we think differently, too."

I push and ask, "How so?"

I'm perplexed when she responds. "My father lives here, too." She explains that he has a place downtown as I wonder why she switches topics and ignores my question about her brother. Why do I feel as though I may have stepped into a minefield? Mental note: "JaRew, check out 'downtown.'"

"Sorry, so what were you saying about your brother? He and your father live downtown?"

"No, just my father. But I was about to say my mother texted me yesterday that she heard Albany is now ranked as one of the state's highest-ranking cities with street violence. So much for my decision to escape violence." Her grimace dilutes her chuckle. Before I respond, she adds, "Hey, you didn't know anything about any of this? The violence? I mean. By the way, what made *you* decide to relocate to Albany?"

"Oh, don't you remember the lead I told you about? Down at the State Legislature." I cross my fingers behind my back.

CHAPTER EIGHTEEN

"How do we fight against violence?"

I'M RELIEVED WHEN Lincoln Cooke, Dez Cooke's uncle, agrees to schedule a meeting to discuss the funds available to support the community's fight against violence. As I hear myself say this, I recognize the irony. How do you fight against violence? Isn't that an oxymoron? Last time I checked, it was.

Beckham had not exaggerated. Lt. Cooke—ex lieutenant—is a good person to know. He hosted the meeting and had sprung for a private banquet room and lunch at an exclusive Italian restaurant. The attendance roster was as impressive as the elite venue's menu. Albany's city council chairperson, the presidents of the Albany NAACP and local police union, were among the attendees. JL's contact, a recently elected young millennial activist from the Bronx, personally attended and shared the approach that she and her staff were using with their community groups.

As we were closing out the meeting, the door unexpectedly opens. We're all shocked since the lieutenant had assured us that we not only had the private room, but the restaurant itself is an off the radar venue.

"Hey, everyone, am I too late for the meeting?"

Yes, you are! I want to scream. JaRew nudges me with his foot under the table, and JL's pen tapping breaks the silence of the otherwise nonresponsive group. I, for one, refuse to allow this meeting and discussion to be reopened. Not with Cooke—*the other Cooke*—in the room. What the heck is he doing here, anyway? I nod at my compadres and begin to gather my notes. JaRew and JL follow my lead. Bingo! Of course, Linc told him about the meeting. I wonder why I'm surprised that he had. My do not trust list is getting as long as my newly touched up human hair weave. Numero uno: Dez Cooke. Numero dos: Beckham. And I'm still not certain of the order. I reserve judgment on the lieutenant as I realize he may be unaware of Beckham's staffing issues. On the other hand, he might now be a part of an inner circle that excludes me. Am I on the outside looking in?

"Hey, Nephew. Yes, you're too late. We just wrapped things up. I'll brief you later."

Before Nephew Cooke can close the door, his uncle thanks the group and says he'll be in touch.

Today might just be the day I bite the bullet and check in with Beckham. Strike while the iron's hot. And I'm hot right now. Linc could have mentioned that his nephew would be joining us. He could have also quite logically assumed that I knew that he was.

Stop it! Blue Lady roars, and I'm glad. I was on a roll and have many more important things to do. Lincoln closes the meeting out, and JaRew, JL, and I exit through the side door.

JL IS HEADING BACK to the Airbnb to work on the grant. I'm now convinced that the three of us will make a great partnership. I also firmly decide to tell Beckham that while I plan to follow through on the

STV project, I'm not happy with his last-minute maneuvering. I'm not naïve, so I *don't* plan to tell him that I'm exploring the possibility of developing a grant proposal myself.

I also know I can't ignore the scope of Lincoln's political and business ties, but based on JL's networking, it looks like we might have a couple of partially opened doors ourselves.

To be honest, I'm scared. I'm petrified. But as I wrestle with my fear, I realize I have to live through it —not back away. I've never backed away from anything before, and I'm too old to start now. I'm going forward with my fear, knowing that if I can withstand it, I will come out on the other side of it. Perhaps a little beaten up, but I plan to withstand the winds of Hurricane Albany and Beckham's wrath if it comes to that. I've lived life long enough to know that what is meant for me is meant for me.

Besides, I'll be getting my first paycheck in a week. That will make me feel a little more confident about the importance of what we're doing. I plan to personally invest it in the Albany community in some way. My tee shirt contribution is a small start and just the beginning. SoS and Marcus are good role models, and I want to follow their lead.

I text my dad regarding the "Shall We Pray" tee shirt project, and he says, "All systems go." Based on our last discussion, that meant they were ordered and would arrive soon.

I smile and do a little happy quick step on my way to the car. "You go, gurl!"

CHAPTER NINETEEN

"Dang, my cover is blown. What do I do now?"

THE VIGIL WILL BE HELD today after the first Saturday morning basketball tournament of the season. The mid-morning game will kick off the weekend for city residents. Family and friends will gather to support their favorite teams knowing that an afternoon of music and good food will follow. JaRew and I will be present, but hopefully unnoticed, blending into the crowd. Our new wardrobes of jeans and more jeans, sweats and tees, and his array of NY Yankees and Nike caps solidify our image. Without a doubt, my big silver hoops are not only my favorite but a most legit accessory. They are perfect for me, Blue Lady—though she won't admit it—and my street life, aka Blue. I cringe every time I think about my 'blue sapphire' blunder. But as they say, it is what it is.

JaRew has done his homework. His increasingly more frequent disappearances are paying off. He has a new running partner after his hookup with DJ G8 at the Big Daddy Kane concert. DJ G8 will mix and spin today. Other than watching and waiting, I can't imagine what JaRew might be doing. I know the DJ invited him to hang out and shoot some hoops with the guys after the game.

S tells me Price Chopper donated a crate of wings, and she's prepared to serve her specialty hot wing combo, as promised. It sounds like her brother let her borrow his food truck and is covering the cost of the condiments, paper products, and fries. I'm really starting to like S. Despite our different backgrounds, we seem to have a lot in common. I was surprised to receive her phone message yesterday. "Hey! I ordered 100 goodie bags for the kids and will bring them with me tomorrow. Oh yeah. My brother is picking up the tab."

I WAIT OUTSIDE the restaurant as S updates her part-timer, telling her business might be slower than usual because of today's events. She lets her know that she can close up shop early if she wants.

JaRew finally checks in with me. He's at the park, but it looks like the day is off to a somber start. The young teenage girl that Marcus told us about is still in critical condition. The local barbershop—someplace called Cutz—was buzzing about the latest turn of events. JaRew and DJ G8 had dropped in to get an edge up before today's activities. I think how awful it must be for people to wake up expecting another day of violence and death.

S shoves some additional supplies in the back of the newly renovated food truck.

"Why didn't you call me to help?"

"No need. You ready for this?"

"Yeah. I guess." Seems like we're feeling about the same. I put on my seat belt as she watches for traffic, exiting the driveway next to her shop. As we head up Madison Avenue, she shares how she's cut her business hours since the violence began. She explains she's just not comfortable in the shop at night anymore. Her brother wants her to sell her pop-up to him. I don't understand why she's not interested. Why do I feel that there are another few pieces to this puzzle?

A PLEASANT-LOOKING elderly woman hugs us as S, and I finally make it to the front of the vendor check-in line.

S's "Hey, Mama Lacy!" is greeted by a loud smooch.

"And this must be Blue." I'm rewarded with an equally loud lip-smacking welcome. Before I can vocalize my thoughts, Mama Lacy reads my mind.

"Pastor Shabazz has told me so much about you."

I smile, return her hug and wonder just how much Pastor Shabazz could have told her since he knows nothing about me. Or does he?

Mama Lacy hands us a multi-colored placard and explains that S can park her food truck in space four and cautions, "Make sure you put your parking permit on your dashboard." She lowers her voice, her right eyebrow arched in non-verbal communication. "Our po-lice will be checkin' for you know who."

The sad part is I know exactly who the "po po" — as Tyler Perry's Madea would say—is "checkin' for."

As I look around, it's hard to believe that the police have to monitor this event. A prayer vigil. Who would think? As though I needed a reality check, a police officer in blue whizzes by with a wave from her police issued scooter. I cringe when I see she's definitely armed. And no one has to tell me that she's probably vested up.

We're early, but it looks like the basketball players are practicing on the court. I think I see JaRew on the backside of the court lugging a huge speaker. The DJ is setting up his equipment. Based on his performance during the breaks between acts at the Kane concert, the crowd is in for some good music and entertainment today.

An outsider may have mistaken the event for a huge outdoor festival based on the setup. Smoke billows from an old whiskey barrel barbecue grill at the backside of the field directly opposite the basketball court. Far enough to allow for the aromatic BBQ flavors to flow throughout the park without burning the eyes of the people traipsing onto the grounds. Attendees smile and chat with each other, most lugging lawn chairs, a few coolers—although, I'd noticed several "No Alcohol Allowed" signs at the entrance to the field. Oblivious to the overall purpose of the event, the frolicking children blow bubbles and spin colorful Frisbees.

As the crowd builds, I see community volunteers in their official-looking blue and white tee shirts and dark jeans circulating alongside the community police officers—a couple of whom are on horseback and are the center of attention. To everyone's surprise, we learn later that more than a thousand people attended the event. Seems like the local churches and other community volunteers did their jobs.

S and I find our designated spot, and I help her set up. We agree that it makes the most sense to have me serve the bottled water and soft drinks from a table outside the food truck where I can also easily pass out the goodie bags to the kids. She'll serve fries and wing baskets from the truck. We'll be ready by the time the game ends. S suggests we look for Marcus to see if he needs any help. We take a few water bottles with us, thinking he and his volunteers might be thirsty. I wrap three in my sweatshirt, and S does the same. We backtrack and take one to Mama Lacy, who smiles and thanks us with a, "Bless you, ladies!"

For some reason, I'm not the least surprised when I see Marcus Pope helping Reverend Shabazz set up a makeshift stage. Marcus had filled S in when he dropped off more flyers. Apparently, a local choir director organized a special community choir to provide spiritual nourishment. The thin, wiry well-dressed man setting up the portable keyboard and sound equipment must be Mr. Edison, the director.

Marcus jumps the few feet off the stage with a solid landing. If I hadn't known who he was, I'd assume he was a local. His denims and Bob Marley Rasta peace shirt were topped off by a black Nike cap, his trademark Ray-Bans, and diamond stud. Reverend Shabazz could have been his twin, except his tee shirt features Stevie Wonder and Martin Luther King and the logo, "Give Peace a Chance." He, too, wears black Nikes.

"Good morning, ladies. Or is it afternoon?"

"Good morning, or I'm in serious trouble." We all laugh at S's cheerful response.

"Hey, Marcus. Hello, Reverend Shabazz. Thirsty?" I reveal my water supply.

"Perfect timing."

Marcus accepts a water bottle and passes it to the reverend. Both their foreheads glisten with slight perspiration.

S notices it, too, and adds, "Looks like you two are working pretty hard over here." She hands them some of the large dinner size white napkins she'd tucked inside her backpack.

"Minister Dennis, want some water?" Marcus yells back at the choir director, who is testing his equipment. He nods, and S trots over with a bottle of water and a few napkins. He, too, is feeling the late morning sun rays. The projected ninety-degree temperatures might become today's reality. Walmart had been more than generous with its water donation. We might run out of ice, though. Volunteers from local churches are setting up rows of chairs in front of the stage.

"What time do you plan to start, Reverend Shabazz?"

He and Marcus outline their plan. Minister Dennis's gospel medley will begin as DJ G8's music mix fades out after the game. Vendors such as we will then begin serving.

Reverend Shabazz will lead off with an opening prayer for peace.

Attendees will eat as the choir sings. Minister Dennis will lead the crowd in his rendition of "We Shall Overcome" as a cadre of children wearing angel wings distribute candles.

The program will conclude with the official candle lighting ceremony and closing prayers.

I'M EXHAUSTED. So is S. My fashion weave has fizzled, and her naturally straight hair is limp, loose, and bodiless. We've already packed the coolers—all empty. The two foldaway tables are stacked against the food truck. We hope that a couple of gentlemen will offer their services. If not, we'll manage. I don't know how S does it. Maybe I'm getting old, but despite how we look, she's ready to party. Her "we deserve it" falls flat. I'm ready all right—for my home away from home comfy double bed. I'd just responded a "great" to JL's text, "How's it going?"

Earlier, JaRew and I passed by each other as strangers in the daylight. I later saw him puffing away on who knows what with his DJ friend and a couple of other guys.

I'm trying to figure out how and when to let S know that I need a rain check. There's no way I'm going to a party. She wants me to meet her brother, and the party is at his house. I have no idea where he lives. Since she intended to drive, I hadn't asked. I'd planned to shower and dress at her apartment. Party hardy was now the last thing I want to do. Shower, most definitely, but at the Airbnb. I won't be surprised if JaRew doesn't make it in tonight. Of course, all in the name of the project, I'm sure. I laugh to myself, thinking, *He works hard. He deserves some R & R.*

Screams block any further thoughts about JaRew's commitment to me and the project. Fear hits my gut as more screams follow. A barrage of what sounds like fireworks in rapid succession destroy the mellow atmosphere that had overtaken the park. Chaos and bedlam reign. Evil threatens to once again destroy a community at peace. And this time, I'm in the middle of it.

Candles that had been lit and placed around the stage flicker in defiance at the red, yellow, and midnight blue fiery bullets that have the power to kill and destroy. The harmonious melodies of peace, love, and let's work together are overpowered by the schizophrenic fusillade of bullets.

Mothers throw their babies to the ground, sacrificing their bodies as non-bulletproof protective armor for the innocent. Husbands do the same for their wives, the loves of their lives. Others crawl or zigzag their way to the parking lots. Sirens, screams, and shouting permeate the night. S and I escape to the food truck.

I don't know who is more frightened, S or me. We're huddled together in the back corner of the truck holding hands, heads touching, faces down. We don't move. Frozen stiff, I feel as though I can hear her heartbeat but realize it's my heart that I'm feeling and her breathing that I'm hearing.

A staccato series of shots shatter the truck's serving window. We tighten our grip in a silent bond and then burst into tears at the loud thud we hear outside. Deadly silence follows. Neither of us wants to know. I weep as my spirit tells me it's probably JaRew. S sniffs and whispers, "Marcus?" I'm embarrassed to realize I feel a wave of relief. Not that I wish it. Her question leads me to think. Reverend Shabazz?

"ANGE? HEY, BLUE. YOU OKAY?" I burst into laughter— hysterical at the relief I feel.

"JaRew?"

Relieved, S and I support each other as we stand up. My knees pop. I'm surprised when JaRew doesn't burst through the door to confirm that I am indeed okay. My legs now tremble as I interpret

JaRew's silence to mean he is alive but wounded. I cover my face. S hugs me. She has no clue who JaRew is, but she witnesses my meltdown. *Dang, my cover is blown. I've got to talk to JaRew. What do I do now?*

I fumble with the locked door. My shaking hands don't cooperate. S shoves me aside and opens the door. JaRew grabs me, saving me from collapsing when I see blood. Blood flows like a raging red river around the crumpled body at the foot of the stairs. I hear S scream, "No!" as I watch JaRew fall, hitting his head on the bottom step.

Blackness surrounds me.

CHAPTER TWENTY

"What do you want with me?"

MY HEAD THROBS. My throat is as dry as a bone. My eyes refuse to open. I sleep.

I wake—my head throbs. I cough. My throat is dry. I need water. I moan. My eyes refuse to open. I sleep.

I wake—my head throbs. I open my eyes. I see blackness. I moan. I sleep.

I wake. I open my eyes. I see blackness. The bed is soft. A soft sheet caresses my neck. I sleep.

I wake. I am no longer alone. I'm afraid to move. Someone adjusts the soft sheet, finds my hand, and holds it. I do not open my eyes. I sleep.

I wake. I open my eyes to bright sunlight and soft music. The tall, handsome, somewhat familiar-looking man places a tray next to the bedside table and leaves the room. I sleep.

I awake this time, hoping the bedside table was not a fantasy. I open my eyes. The tray remains untouched, covered with a crisp white linen napkin. A white ceramic carafe and crystal goblet of iced water remind me of my thirst. I close my eyes, but my thirst is stronger than my desire to return to the blackness in which I have up to now found comforting. The door opens.

I close my eyes.

"WHAT DO YOU WANT WITH ME?"

He doesn't answer but attempts to get me to eat. Toast? *I hate white bread.*

"Leave me alone. What do you want?"

He doesn't answer but hands me a glass of water.

I slap it away. The goblet falls and crashes on the inlaid marble floor. I conclude that I'm dreaming.

When he brushes my hair from my face, I know his touch is real. It actually *feels* familiar. But how could it?

I refuse to cry. "What...do...you...want?"

"You." He lays a red robe and slippers across an off-white cushioned lounge chair.

"Why don't you take a shower? I bet you'll feel better."

Frightened. I wait to hear that he's truly locked the bedroom door, his usual practice, and get up, hoping my phone is still in my pocket. My jeans are nowhere to be found. *Duh*! *You really think he'd leave you with a phone?*

"Shut up, Blue Lady. Now is not the time." Although I angrily dismiss her, I'm relieved to hear her voice. A poignant reminder that I'm okay.

I realize I'm wearing a short black silk nightshirt. I don't want to think about the fact that this stranger has seen what he's had no right to see. I cover my mouth to prevent myself from screaming and lightly touch my body for evidence that he's done the unspeakable.

He hasn't.

What does he want with me?

How long have I been here?

Where is "here?" *Who* is 'he'?

Suddenly, I remember JaRew. I see the blood. Two bodies. Not just one. Oh my God, where's S? Last I remember, we were together. She was fine. I was fine. JaRew—he called my name, and... My mind is blank. I fight the tears, wipe my eyes, and Blue Lady reminds me. *Now, think! What are "we" going to do?*

"We" decide to risk taking a shower. I check the door. It's locked. I'm shocked when I look around. I feel like I'm in a Five Diamond hotel. I have to step down into the glass-enclosed circular shower. The crimson red vanity and sunken tub make me feel as though I'm still dreaming, but the warmth from the heated floor tells me otherwise. Matching his and her sinks are laced with assorted amenities. I ignore the implications, quickly take a shower, unable to savor the luxurious setting. For the first time, I wonder if I'm still in Albany. I shiver at the possibility that I'm not. I brush my teeth and hair with my eyes closed. I don't want to look at myself in the mirror.

"HEY, BLUE..."

Blue Lady's MISSION under FIRE

I have visitors. Shocked is not the word, but I can't think of another. Blown away, perhaps. Blue Lady suggests, *Pissed.* I refuse to go there.

S and my mysterious caretaker are waiting for my re-entrance, sitting side by side on the luxury lounge chair. Now, I understand why he looks so familiar.

He and S have the same deep-set pronounced eyes —his slightly larger than hers. Hers are as red and swollen as mine feel—his clear and bright.

His hair is just as black and straight as hers. His, edged and gelled. Hers, dull and in need of a good brushing.

He's lean, lanky, and muscular. She's lean, toned, and not as tall.

I claim my seat on the king-sized bed that appears to have fresh linens and newly fluffed pillows and plan to wait it out as I figure it out.

"Do you feel better, Blue?"

I don't answer. Blue Lady chides, *Oh, so now, you remember him? What is wrong with you? Be for real. I can't believe it's taken you so long to figure this out. And you still want to trust her? Ha!*

The so-called player has been played. So much for my undercover efforts. Beckham was right. Now, I understand. He had no choice but to bring in Dez Cooke once the demonstration piece was added to the project. I'd been suckered by the very first person I met.

Blue Lady pipes up, *Maybe you should let me do the talking.* I nod my head. S thinks I'm acknowledging her. I decide to play dumb, and as I think about it, it seems that dumb is what I've been. *No comments.*

Blue Lady takes the floor, and I hope I won't regret my decision.

"So, what's this all about, Siracchi?" She uses her last name, making it clear that friendship is no longer an option. "What do you and your brother want with me?" Her brother responds on her behalf.

"Please don't blame her."

"Why not?" Blue Lady asks. "And please don't tell me that you're not her brother!"

S speaks for herself. "He *is* my brother. Why would I lie about that? We had plans to go to his party last night. Remember?"

Blue Lady's MISSION under FIRE

I remember, but she has a lot of explaining to do. When I think about how gullible I've been, I'm ready to cry. Mid sniff, my stomach jerks. I grab it, feeling as though I've been sucker punched. *Don't you dare cry. And you have been sucker-punched.*

Blue Lady screeches and approaches Siracchi as though she intends to return the favor on my behalf. I decide it's time for me to step up and do what I need to do, but before I can speak, I think, Oh, no! Don't tell she's part of the plan.

Can you hold on and let me do this? You really don't get it, do you?

I ignore Blue Lady and speak for myself. "How did I get here? And...and, what do you want with me?" Oh, Lord, I stop before I totally lose it.

Blue Lady yells and throws in a few curse words for emphasis. "Siracchi, what's going on? How did I get here? And what does your brother want with me?"

"I'm sorry. I really am." She starts to cry. "I really don't know." She looks at her brother. "Sincere, what's the deal? What's going on? You promised —"

"That's enough." Her brother yells and turns to leave us alone in the bedroom. "I'm ordering dinner. S, text me your orders." We ignore him as the door once again closes.

S apologizes for what seems like the hundredth time. She says she doesn't know what her brother wants with me and affirms that she'd really planned for us to attend his party—he'd asked her to bring me.

When I ask how she knew I was at his house, she looks at the floor and doesn't respond. Rather than press her now and face the possibility that she'll lie to me, I change the subject. *Why are you not pressing for answers?* I ignore Blue for now.

"How did you get home last night?"

Again, she refuses to look at me. I have no doubt that she realizes her eyes are the windows to her soul. *You're right on this one. She's lying. What is she not telling you?*

"I drove."

"And the bodies?" I yell. "And what happened to the two dead guys?" I cringe at the words, but I

167

not only need to know, I need to know just how much she knows.

"Nobody died last night."

I don't believe her. Blue Lady intervenes before I can stop her. "Be for real, Siracchi. Two bodies were on the ground outside your brother's food truck.

"Ten wounded. No deaths." She shakes her head and bursts into tears. "I left right after you..."

"You left? What do you mean?"

"I was afraid."

I'm relieved to hear that there were no deaths, but I'm concerned about JaRew. I've got to get out of here. Blue Lady reminds me I need to be smart and not stupid.

"Get me out of here, S." I don't like the look she gives me. Something's definitely wrong.

I hear the lock turn. The door opens. Sincere smiles. How can someone so evil look like an angel? "Do you promise to have a cocktail with me if I let you talk to Jarewski? Think about it." He turns to leave. "Dinner will be here in about twenty minutes."

CHAPTER TWENTY-ONE

"How do you play the game called life?"

SIRACCHI REMINDS me that she'd already shared her concerns about her brother and his lifestyle with me. She ignores my inquiring eyebrows and shrugs her shoulders. Simply said, she tells me her brother is attracted to me and that he won't do anything to harm me. When I burst into semi-hysterical laughter, she does too. I feel like I'm really losing it but listen as she proceeds to fill me in on the details of last night... So she says.

When I didn't respond when she called me, she'd peeked out the broken food truck window and glimpsed a man running across the backfield with a body—presumably mine—over his shoulder. She saw him open the back door of his vehicle and place me in the back seat. He roared off. With further prodding, she shamefully admits that she recognized the car. It belongs to some guy named Five who works for her brother.

The more S tells me about the situation, the more I realize I have to make some serious decisions. Blue Lady has already cautioned me to go slow and dig deep. She reminds me I'm playing the game called life in a city with unpredictable odds and where the numbers are definitely stacked against me. I have to keep my cards close to my chest, maintain a poker face, and forget about trusting anyone.

I realize S just might be my most valuable asset. I need to know how and what her brother knows about JaRew. *Don't ask her. Wait her out. Don't worry, she'll mention his name if she's legit.* I know Blue Lady is right.

I'm locked in a room against my wishes in an unknown location by a man I don't really know. I don't know how I got here or who brought me. I realize I really don't know much of anything. But I do know that the only person I have contact with is someone I've known for less than a month and who just happens to be the sister of the man who has me under lock and key. Blue Lady reminds me that this man is also the one who taught me the cubic shuffle and convinced me to do Tequila shots. Memories of that hot sultry evening resurface, but I shove them aside as quickly as they had appeared. My subconscious ignores my efforts to dismiss reality and reminds me of the warm body that lay next to me last night, the soft touch of the hands that adjusted the silk sheets under my chin and the sexy voice that whispered, "You can trust me, Blue." I hear that same sensuous voice, "I'd say chug it—like this!"

The shots. What was in the shots?

"I dare you."

S then says I should take her brother up on his offer. She then asks, "By the way, who *is* Jarewski?" I don't respond. Blue Lady says, *Humph, I told you.*

I confirm. "So, you think I should take your brother up on this plan of his?"

She smiles and winks. "I do. He *really* likes you."

Blue Lady pokes me. *Be careful. Why is she just telling you this? More importantly, what is she not telling you?*

"But what does he plan to do with me?" I can't help but wonder how much Sincere knows about Jarewski.

Or me.

CHAPTER TWENTY-TWO

"Oh, God, what am I supposed to do?"

S GIVES ME A QUICK HUG, assures me that I'll be fine, and she'll be back later. She wants to shower and change and has some business to take care of. *Like what?* I ignore Blue Lady's nudge. As an afterthought, S whispers, "He really likes you, Ange." I don't answer because this is something I can't fathom.

NO ONE WOULD BELIEVE me if I told them that I'm being held against my will, under lock and key, sipping my second mimosa. To further complicate matters, the cocktails were hand made just for me by a very handsome and charming guy who toasted "to us" with a click against the crystal goblet from which I sip. A familiar voice hisses, *How quickly we forget.*

I've adjusted to the bedroom suite and my view of the river from the patio window. I haven't figured out exactly where I am, but from what I've learned about the area, I guess I'm in one of the several small towns northwest of the city. I miss having my phone, but for some bizarre reason, I'm no longer worried about my personal safety.

Courtesy of Sincere, I've talked to JaRew, and the two of us share our relief at knowing that we're each okay. My keeper abruptly ends the call when an unfamiliar voice with a New York accent pipes up, "Yo, man, I'll see you in a few."

Sincere's piercing stare fails at its attempt to mesmerize me, although his deep voice caresses my name. "Blue, your friend will be here in about ten minutes. Do you want to get dressed? I bought you a new outfit."

OTHER THAN THE dark circles under my eyes, I'm fine—physically. I parted my hair in the middle and twisted it into two thick French braids. I've never worn Gucci sweats, but I must admit, the designer sweat suit fits me well. *He knows your size. And he's discovered your style.*

The matching slides are not only cute but more comfortable than the Nike sneakers S had insisted I buy to wear to the vigil. And I can't ignore Blue Lady's astute observation. He's somehow discovered my predilection for designer lines. But it will take a lot more than a Gucci sweat suit to get over on me. *You can always let him think that he has.*

Sincere and Five, JaRew's bodyguard, disappear, leaving JaRew and me in the informal dining area off the kitchen. I discover that Five is not only the owner of the NYC accent but also Sincere's right-hand man— and my kidnapper. I later learn that he befriended JaRew at the barbershop. Yes, Cutz, one of Sincere's many businesses.

Sincere makes it a point to refill my goblet and offer JaRew a beer. JaRew cold-shoulders the offer. I nervously pretend to sip the frothy drink and glance at Sincere. He shrugs his shoulders and strolls out of the room. Soft, smooth surround sound jazz replaces the silence.

Other than a bruised right shoulder, massive headache, and a huge lump on the back of his head, JaRew tells me he's quite well. My eyes tear when I think that he could have died trying to save me. "Tell me, who did this to you?"

He shushes me with his finger, nodding toward the other room. His foot jabs mine. He asks, "So, who's this guy? How do you know him?"

I can't tell if he's serious or if he's playing games since his foot is creeping up my leg now, well past my ankle.

I respond louder than usual. Blue Lady's punch to my chest competes with JaRew's poke at my knee. I whisper, "Where am I?" JaRew shakes his head.

I don't want to think about what we've both been through or what happens next. Sincere has made it clear that my guest has a fifteen-minute visitation slot.

"How are you?"

"I'm okay. You?"

He pokes me again. "Where's your friend?"

I'm not sure what he saw last night or how much he knows. I hope my peeked eyebrows sufficiently respond for me.

"The young lady that you were helping out yesterday?"

I play it safe. "I don't know." I lean over, and he pokes me harder. *Don't do it!* Blue Lady screams.

He now has his foot on top of my knee. I feel a lump.

Oh, God, what am I supposed to do?

"Are you sure you're okay?"

I nod, and before I can say anything, Sincere pokes his head in. "Eight more minutes. And no funny stuff."

JaRew lowers his eyes, blinks, and presses his foot again on top of my knee. *He's trying to give you something, Girl,* Blue Lady whispers. I slowly lower my left hand beneath the table while sipping from my drink with my right.

Blue Lady is right on it. I slide a small box-like item from his sock and lay it between my thighs and adjust my shirt. He reaches for my hand across the table. I'm shocked not only by the move, but by

Sincere's, "Okay, man, this visit is over. Five, time to go." Five enters the room, heading toward JaRew.

JaRew stands and pushes Five's hand off his shoulder. "No need for that—I heard him. I'm ready.

Let's go."

Sincere separates the two. "All right, all right! Cut it!

This is not the time. Or the place."

Together they walk JaRew to the door. I see Five handcuff him. "Take care of yourself, Blue. I'll see you when I see you."

"And that won't be anytime soon, man." Sincere slams the door. I walk back to the bedroom. The reciprocating slam of the door speaks for me. And this time, *I* turn on the lock. Tears escape. Blue Lady does nothing to stop me or my tears.

CHAPTER TWENTY-THREE

"What do I do? Who do I call?"

I SIT AND WAIT, not at all sure what to do. Beckham was right. I'm not cut out for this kind of stuff. Will you please stop it? What happened to "I can do all things?" "No mountain is too high?" "I have to do what I have to do to get where I got to go?" How quickly we forget. So, cut the crap!

All right, all right! I got it.

Just as I think Sincere might have left, I hear footsteps and shove the phone under the cushion. So, I have a phone. What good is it? Who am I to call? 911? *It's better than just shoving your lifeline under the lounge chair cushion.*

I can't think. What do I do? Who do I call? *No, not your father, Ange. C'mon. We can do this.*

I'm so glad I locked the door, but I know in my heart that no lock in the world will stop this man. He's on a mission. I don't know his purpose, but I'm a part of the plan. I sit, frozen, praying for some sense of direction. *Smart move.*

"Are you okay?"

Sincere's voice actually sounds sincere. If I didn't know better, I would think that he's seriously concerned about me.

I'm not surprised at all when the knob turns, and the massive door swings open as though in response to his silent command. *Remote control, huh? He is indeed as smooth as a silky, velvety wine. Humph.*

Sincere joins me on the lounge chair that is more than large enough for both of us. In a series of synchronized moves, he slides the throw pillow under my head, relaxes and adjusts his lean but muscular body to fit mine, and spreads the matching satin comforter over the two of us. We lay silently.

"I've never met anyone like you before, Blue." I don't answer.

"Is that your real name?"

"Why?"

"I just want to know." I sigh.

"You don't have to be afraid of me, Angelica."

I sigh again. My eyes close as though seeing is believing, and that my temporary blindness will obliterate Sincere's cavalier, but so sincere, sounding revelation.

"You know my name?"

"Of course, I do. I know everything about you, Angelica Mason, MPA. Smoothville City Operations Manager. University of Georgia graduate. Shall I go on?"

I pray for the right words. Blue Lady is silent. I'm tempted to say yes, go on. Tell me what else you know.

"You don't have to be afraid of me." Why does he think repetitious meaningless words will eliminate my fear? Why should I trust him?

Before Blue Lady says something I wouldn't, I decide to confront this man who dares to tell me not to be afraid as he holds me captive.

"What do you take me for? I didn't graduate magna cum laude because I was stupid, you know."

I pull my hand away as he tries to hold it.

"What do you want from me?"

He scoots even closer, laying his chin on my head and gently strokes my hand. I don't recognize the scent, but the musky floral notes of his cologne are as bold as the masculinity of his move. I shiver at his soft touch, brush his hand away and chide myself at my woeful attempt to snub him. Instead, I turn to face him, searching his eyes for meaning. I discover pleading.

"I want you to get to know me. I want you to give me a chance to let you know how much I want to be with you. I want you to—"

Sincere's sanctuary is no longer sacred... The specialty, precision-made bedroom door splinters under 700 plus pounds of weight and specially designed SWAT equipment. Three Glocks dare us to move. Sincere freezes behind me on the lounger, but bellows, "Let her go. I'm the one you want."

Dez Cooke, Linc, and a uniformed officer remain in position—ominous, unmovable, and as solid as the MLK memorial statute. I don't budge. I couldn't if I tried. Sincere whispers, "You're free, Blue. Go."

I turn to look at him. He kisses me on the nape of my neck. "Go. Please. I don't want anything to happen to you."

Dez Cooke walks across the room with his gun aimed at Sincere's head.

"Move it, man. Let her go."

Sincere nudges me away. Linc walks over to get me, takes my hand, and shoves me behind him, never missing a beat. He, too, points his ugly black gun at my captor.

I barely make it across the room when an unarmed but vested Jarewski breaks the lock on the patio door with a sledgehammer, grabs Sincere, and lands a perfect right hook crushing the button of Sincere's nose. The uniformed officer grabs Sincere and handcuffs him as blood continues to spurt from his nostrils. Cooke steps in front of JaRew eradicating any further plans he might have.

Sincere refuses to look at me as he's handcuffed and escorted from the room. I don't know which, but one of the officers somberly performs his duty. "You have the right to remain silent..."

Blue Lady's MISSION under FIRE

JL, JAREW, and I are huddled around JL's sister's kitchen table in Westchester County. Since we didn't know who to trust, we returned our rental, switched it out for another vehicle in JL's name, and headed downstate. We need time to regroup, reassess, and decide the next steps.

I'm exhausted. JL is clueless. JaRew is JaRew. His hand is bandaged but not broken. He fills us in — qualifying the accuracy of the information he shares because, with only a few exceptions, it's totally secondhand. He had relied on Dez Cooke and his uncle for most of it.

JaRew overlooks his intervention steps as though they had not occurred. He shared that he wasn't certain just how much Beckham might know about the unusual turn of events. Neither Cooke reached out to him, but he indicated that he had no doubt that both had filled in Beckham.

Per JaRew, Dez Cooke was the other body outside the food truck. He'd been tailing JaRew and me at the vigil. He'd run into Marcus Pope after the grant meeting. Marcus told him about the vigil and that I was helping him out. When panic broke out at the event, JaRew easily tracked me to the food truck since he'd been watching my every move all afternoon.

When he called my name to ensure I was indeed okay after the shots were fired into the truck, Five arrived because Sincere had heard about the shootings and sent him to make sure I was safe. Five approached the truck as JaRew was about to enter, hit him over the head, only to be attacked by Cooke. When Dez pulled out his gun to shoot Five, Five kicked it out of his hand and body-slammed him. Five decided to give Cooke something to remember him by. He confiscated Cooke's gun, fired off a shot—one that glazed his leg only to use the same weapon to crack JaRew over the head. With no weapon and an injured leg, Cooke played possum. Both Cooke and JaRew were discovered by local police in the aftermath of the shootings. Cooke's injury caused him to lose a lot of blood but had not resulted in major damage. He and JaRew were taken by ambulance to the ER and released.

Five had grabbed me, wrapped me up in a hooded cape, threw me over his shoulder, and taken me to his boss. Courtesy of Sincere, multiple dosages of over-the-counter sleep meds knocked me out for the count.

"So, how much did your friend Siracchi know about this?"

I sigh. "That's a problem. I don't know."

"Did you ask her?"

"I haven't talked to her since her brother was arrested."

They both look at me, waiting for me to say more.

"Have you talked to Beckham?"

"No." I look at my nails as though they've whispered my name.

They wait for me to respond. I haven't thought this through, and a part of me wants to say that, but I realize if I'm going to lead this group, I have to step to the plate and take it head-on. I go for it.

"Other than my parents, you guys are the only people I trust. I think we make a great team. I accept that this project is nothing like I thought it would be." I hesitate but continue. "Beckham may have been right when he decided that I was not the best person to lead the STV initiative." JaRew began to interrupt, but I need to finish.

"Please hear me out, JaRew. By acknowledging that, I don't mean to imply that he handled it in the right way. He didn't. As the administrator of the grant, he should have been comfortable sharing his logic with me." I laugh. "You guys know me, so I'm not saying I would have accepted his thinking any more readily than I did at the onset and even now as this project seems to have fallen apart."

We chuckle, and JL's sister, Daira, tiptoes in and leaves a tray of snacks on the table. JL goes to the kitchen for drinks. JaRew plays one of his many phone games.

This time, JL has a point. She raises her hand as though a student in class.

Although I shake my head and place my finger against my lips—"one minute, please"—I sit, unsure of what I should say. I also wonder what SoS is doing. And I can't help but think about Sincere. I know better than to share these thoughts—at least, not now. But if I plan to propose a business relationship that will succeed because of our trust in each other to be the best partners we can be, I know I will have to share my feelings on what awaits us in Albany.

If my partners agree, we will return to Albany. Our mission may be under fire, but it's not over.

Since I haven't spoken, JL risks a question. "Do you think we can trust Dez Cooke?"

I'm surprised when JaRew looks up from his game. "I don't know. Maybe"

"I still have my suspicions. Why, JL?"

"I don't know. I have a feeling he's on the right track."

"What about Hinkley?" Unanimous vote. "No!" "Marcus?" I ask.

"Yes!" Another unanimous vote.

"I guess there's hope for us then!"

JaRew stands up as though leaving. I wonder why he's changing his mind.

"What's wrong? Where are you going, JaRew?"

"To get my laptop. We've got work to do."

"Yep, we do."

"Let's brainstorm about our business model."
"Sounds good. What about our company name?"
"Definitely," JL adds.

"And our first official mission?"

"Give peace a chance?" Perfect!

THE END

Many Thanks for choosing to read **Blue Lady's MISSION under FIRE**. I truly appreciate it. If you enjoyed it, please consider writing a review on the site where you purchased it. (Short ones are fine and quite welcome.)

If you'd like to be notified of my new releases, please sign up at my website: https://www.stephany-tullis.com.

By now, I know you won't be the least bit surprised when I share that Angelica is off and running. Again. But this time, is she running away from or towards the journey of a life time? Has she truly decided to give peace a chance? Please get your copy of Blue Lady's DÉJÀ VU on the Seas at https://books2read.com/u/3J6RGE

INTRODUCTION AND EXCERPT

It's all about the search for love and life purpose...

Blue Lady's DÉJÀ VU on the Seas is Book 4 in *The Angelica Mason Series* (There are four books in this series). Book 5, Blue Lady's SEARCH for LOVE will be available in the Spring of 2023). The books revolve around a common theme—the search for love and life purpose.

Which is more important or are they interrelated?

Which takes more courage—ignoring the fear or staring it in the face?

Blue Lady's MISSION under FIRE

In Book 4, Déjà Vu on the Seas, Angelica Mason embarks on a journey of a life time; one that is full of unknowns but with her commitment to search and prepare to accept whatever she finds.

Angelica is known in political circles for her highly effective 'do it my way or hit the highway' MO. Not one to be intimidated, she's never second-guessed herself. Once she's made up her mind, she perseveres to the finish. No regrets. Until now.

Traumatized by several near-death experiences, including a kidnapping, Angelica returns to her safe place and finds the security she so desperately needs in her king size bed. There, she succumbs to the dense fog that has smothered her spirit.

And sleeps.

Frightened when her BFF doesn't return her phone calls or text messages, Nicole Honeywell makes a surprise visit to check in on her missing in action childhood friend. Nicole is alarmed by Angelica's bedridden, bedraggled and semi-comatose condition. When she threatens to sound the alarm and contact Angelica's business partner and parents if Angelica doesn't get her act together, Angelica sluggishly promises to do so.

She's only awake long enough to ascertain two things.

Something's seriously wrong.

And she needs to do something about it.

But rather than take the chance that she'll be bombarded with unwanted visitors making unmeetable demands, she accepts her only alternative.

Escape.

PROLOGUE

"The beginning of the end…"

NOTHING INTIMIDATED Ms. Angelica Marie Mason, and she never second-guessed herself. Once she made up her mind, she persevered to the finish. No regrets. Not one iota of remorse even when she impetuously decided to leave her prestigious position at the country's powerhouse in Washington, DC and return to her childhood home in Smoothville, Georgia. Angelica had learned a lot, enjoyed her experience and made several good friends, including her mentor, Dr. Beckham Johnson.

No one asked, and Angelica felt no need to share how, why, or when she consciously decided to no longer interpret the maneuvers and machinations of DC's decision makers. As with most other critical lifetime events, the date and details were etched in her mind: Monday, January first at 6:00 p.m.

And on February first at 6:45 a.m., instead of heading to the DC Metro, she hopped into her newly financed Audi RS Q3 and drove downtown to another capitol building, Smoothville City Hall. Angelica easily readjusted to small town living without missing a beat, and via a combination of luck, bumping heads with the right people, and her DC experience, she made the perfect landing.

As with DC, she quickly made a name for herself. Smoothville mayor, Luke Evans, was the first to experience Angelica's no-nonsense highly effective work style and ethic. No one could convince him otherwise—he had first-hand experience. Angelica Mason "was no joke." She had more than proved herself when she salvaged him and his election a few years ago from his self-inflicted political wounds. Evans acknowledged to his supporters, friends, and family—even to his public audience—that he'd made some serious mistakes and assured them that he had learned his lessons—the hard way. He promised his mistakes would never be repeated. Little did Angelica know that the Luke Evans she trusted would someday renege on his commitments, including the vow he made to her.

TWO YEARS AGO, Angelica's father, Marshall Mason who was never sick a day in his life—not even with a bad cold—scared the crapola out of her when he had a massive heart attack. Angelica's otherwise super sophisticated and self-acknowledged bougie mother, Marilyn Mason, hysterically broke the news at 2:00 a.m. from the Savannah General Hospital emergency room.

By 7:00 a.m., a somber hold her own, not frightened by much, Angelica was at her father's bedside, struggling to hold back tears. Her mother sobbed enough for the two of them. Sophistication was no longer on the table. Marilyn's no makeup appearance made that clear.

Marshall Mason's heart attack was much more than Angelica's first exposure to death. No one had to tell her how ill her father was. "Massive heart attack" was a fully loaded, much-too-commonly-used medical term that didn't require extensive research to determine the severity of the diagnosis nor the potential impacts. She fought against all those possibilities with every bone in her body, resisting the mind games that played with her emotions.

The personal strength and stamina that most saw and admired rallied to the forefront. When family friend, Dr. Bryant, met with the family to gravely review Marshall's health status and prognosis, Angelica did what she knew she had to do.

WITHOUT A SECOND THOUGHT, Angelica messaged her boss. "Luke, I need to take a leave of absence." The mayor honored her request, but she would have quit her job, if necessary. Her father assured her that he'd be okay. "Marilyn and I will find a way." His body language and tone confirmed what she already knew. He'd find a way. But there would be no way that would meet 'Mother Dear's' exacting standards—something they both knew. Angelica stepped to the plate. She made a quick trip back to Smoothville, grabbed her laptop, some underwear, toiletries, and sweats and was back in time to drive her parents from the hospital to her home away from home—their recently purchased pre-retirement home.

SHE'D JUST RETURNED FROM a celebratory dinner with her father where he promised her: no fried chicken, no more than one whiskey on the rocks a month—and only to celebrate something special— to drink more tea than coffee, and renew his gym membership when she got the call. Her long-time colleague, point person, and now good friend Jonathan C. Jarewski—aka JaRew— broke the news.

"Hey, your ex, Lover Boy, is now sitting in your corner office with his personalized shiny new name plate on the door.

"That scumbag of a boss of ours reassigned me to Communications, the job I told you I'd never perform again, even if my life depended on it, and get this, I came to work today, but guess where my office is? That cold, gloomy, windowless back room in the basement." In typical Jarewski style, he paused for effect and added, "By the way, I quit."

But quick as a whip, Angelica had a new job before collecting her first unemployment check. Beckham Johnson's timing couldn't have been more perfect. He'd coincidently reached out to Angelica to chat and get an update on her dad's health status. Angelica shared that her father was great and recently released from his doctor's care but that her boss had just fired her. Without hesitation, excited at the opportunity to work with her again, he chimed, "Hey Angelica, guess what? I need a project manager, and I'd love for it to be you."

Voilà! Angelica not only had a new job but had worked a deal with Beckham to have JaRew on her project team. She eagerly looked forward to the new position, viewing it as the next fork in the road—one that would lead to another step up the ladder. More importantly, she believed it was definitely a "sign" that Shawn Mallory, the ex that had just stolen her job, was definitely a "fling" of the past.

Little did she know that her new project would expose her to a cloak and dagger new world—a 21st century urban Twilight Zone.

Angelica walked and talked it as best as she could for two months—twenty-four hours a day.

She lived it. Immersed herself in it.

She escaped it. But barely.

Actually, she was mercifully rescued. Some might say, JaRew saved the day; others, that he literally saved her life.

Was she mercifully rescued? Did JaRew save the day? Want to know the answer? Grab your copy of Blue Lady's DÉJÀ VU on the Seas.

ABOUT THE AUTHOR

Stephany Tullis is the USA Today and Amazon bestselling author of character-driven edgy inspirational fiction. Whether inspirational, contemporary or women's fiction, her books center around love, hope and second chances. Her small-town romances revolve around love and forgiveness examining issues common to today's lifestyle and relationships.

Stephany grew up in upstate New York and fell in love with books on her first trip to the library, influenced by her mother who was an avid reader!

Her motto, 'writing with purpose', reflects her intent to have her stories not only entertain readers but to inspire and uplift their spirits. Her readers write: "As is the norm with this author, she has a firm grasp on human nature and what makes them (people) tick.

Stephany is energized by the sun, thrives on music (all genres) and is inspired by the serenity of the ocean. She loves to travel and summer is her season. Beach-based outdoor music festivals allow her to creatively combine these interests.

To connect with Stephany and learn about her books…

Facebook: https://www.facebook.com/StephanyTullis2
Twitter: https://twitter.com/StephanyTullis
Instagram: https://www.instagram.com/stephanytullis/
Pinterest:
https://www.pinterest.com/stephanytwrites/_created/
Website: https://www.stephany-tullis.com/
Bookbub: https://www.bookbub.com/authors/stephany-tullis
Amazon: https://www.amazon.com/Stephany-Tullis/e/B00D3P052W

OTHER BOOKS BY STEPHANY TULLIS

CONTEMPORARY WOMEN'S FICTION
The Angelica Mason Series

BLUE LADY (Prequel)

Blue Lady's SWEET DREAMS, Book 2

Blue Lady's MISSION under FIRE, Book 3

Blue Lady's DÉJÀ VU on the Seas, Book 4 (A Short Story)

Blue Lady's SEARCH for LOVE, Book 5
(Available Spring 2023)

INSPIRATIONAL WOMEN'S FICTION
The Miracle Circle Series

The Master's Plan, A Novel, Book 1

48 Hours 'Til Christmas, Book 2

Blue Lady's MISSION under FIRE

WOMEN'S CONTEMPORARY ROMANCE
The What Love Can Do Series

Love Rescues, Book 1
Love Strengthens, Book 2
Love Understands, Book 3 (To be available in 2023)

NEW INSPIRATIONAL FICTION SERIES

Angels of Grace

In the Beginning, Book 1 (Available 2023)

NONFICTION

My Soul Speaks: *Who am I?* (Available February 2023)

Blue Lady's MISSION under FIRE